SPIRIT HUNTERS

SOMETHING
WICKED

Also by Ellen Oh

Spirit Hunters
Spirit Hunters: The Island of Monsters
Finding Junie Kim
The Dragon Egg Princess
A Thousand Beginnings and Endings
(Edited by Ellen Oh and Elsie Chapman)
Prophecy
Warrior
King

ELLEN OH

SPIRIT HUNTERS

SOMETHING WICKED

HARPER
An Imprint of HarperCollinsPublishers

Library of Congress Control Number: 2022934037
ISBN 978-0-06-298801-0

Typography by Andrea Vandergrift
22 23 24 25 26   PC/LSCH   10 9 8 7 6 5 4 3 2 1
❖
First Edition

This book is for all the readers who like to stay up late reading scary books, and then have to hold their pee all night because the hallway to the bathroom seems ever so far, and ever so dark, and there's definitely something lurking out there, waiting to . . .

CHANGES

The cold wind blew in Harper Raine's face, drying out her eyes as she rode her bike back to her house. She'd been over at her friend Dayo's house for a sleepover and was on her way home after a large, fantastic breakfast of pancakes and eggs and bacon. Harper had eaten so much food she'd ended up walking her bike at first while Dayo laughed and waved her off. But as the cold December morning penetrated Harper's heavy black coat, she'd jumped on her bike to get home as fast as possible.

Walking up to her house, Harper spied a small package at her front door. She picked it up and saw it was addressed to her mom.

"Hey, Mom! You got a package," Harper yelled as she slammed the door shut.

Immediately, she heard the thundering steps of her older sister running down the stairs and barreling toward her.

"It's my K-beauty supplies!" Kelly shrieked as she snatched the box from Harper's hands and did a weird little jig. She tore through the packaging and pulled out a bag full of Korean beauty face masks in all different colors. Harper peered over her shoulder in curiosity.

"Snail mucus?" Harper gagged. "You're gonna put that on your face?"

With a nasty glare, Kelly shoved past her. "What do you know about anything?"

"I know I wouldn't put no stinky snail slime on my face!"

Ignoring her, Kelly ran into the living room, where her mother was sitting with Michael reading a book.

"Mom, I got all the special skin care masks! Let's do a beauty night!" Dumping them onto the coffee table, Kelly fanned them out into a big colorful display.

"Mm-hmm," her mother responded absently.

"Shhh, Kelly! I'm reading to Mommy!" Michael said.

"Sorry," Kelly replied. Sweeping the beauty masks back into her box, she made her way toward the stairs. "I'll be in my room."

By the time Harper had hung up her coat and scarf and come into the living room, Kelly was gone.

"Harper, you sit and listen," Michael commanded.

"Yes, sir." She immediately went to sit in her father's brand-new recliner but stopped to see two scrawny feet sticking up in the air.

"Aw, come on, Leo, I want to sit in it!"

"Too bad, so sad."

Huffing in irritation, Harper dropped her backpack on the floor and plopped down on the thick rug in front of the toasty fire. Leo was her cousin on her father's side. His mother was Harper's father's younger sister. She was the hotel manager at the Grande Bennington Hotel Resort and Beach Club on Razu Island, while Leo's father was the head pastry chef at the same hotel. After their vacation on the island and all the weirdness that happened there, Aunt Caroline had asked Harper's parents to let Leo live with them and attend public school. At least that was the reason her parents gave when Leo moved in.

But Harper had overheard them talking about how bad they felt for Leo now that his parents were getting a divorce and fighting over everything.

Biting back the sharp retort teetering at the tip of her tongue, Harper sighed. While she and Leo had gotten closer due to their time on the island, it was still weird having him living with them instead of just visiting. Taking up space everywhere, like sitting in the new armchair that Harper loved.

"When's Grandma coming back?" she asked peevishly.

"I know you miss her, honey, but a broken hip takes a very long time to heal," her mother replied. "And her doctor doesn't want her to be moved for several more weeks. It's doubtful that she'll even be home for Christmas."

Grandma Lee had been visiting Harper's aunt Youjin in New York when she fell and broke her hip. That had been during Halloween, over five weeks ago. Now it was December and Grandma was still not home. It made Harper antsy. While Harper had gone up to visit her grandmother twice already, it wasn't the same. First off, Grandma was confined to a bed in her aunt's house. Second, there was hardly any time to speak privately with her, what with everyone oohing and aahing over Aunt Youjin's new baby.

Harper had spent most of her time cuddling Monty, Grandma's Yorkie. Little Monty was super cute but very distracting. There was so much she wanted to show her grandma, but the timing was never quite right.

"When can we go see Grandma again?" she asked.

"We're definitely going to go up during winter break," her mother replied.

"Winter break? But that's the end of the month!"

"I know, honey, but your dad and I have far too much work this month and won't be able to go up before then."

"Poor Grandma," Michael said in his sweet little voice. "She will be so boring without us."

"Bored, not boring," Leo responded.

"That's what I said, bored-ing."

Harper giggled and then let out a painful gasp when Michael jumped onto her stomach.

"Harper did you bringded me some of Dayo's cookies?"

"I don't know, Michael, what's 'bringded' mean?"

"Bring me! Bring me!" Michael shouted.

"May-be yes, may-be no."

"Harper!"

"May-be in my backpack."

Bouncing off Harper's stomach, Michael opened Harper's bag and crowed in delight to find a Ziploc full of Dayo's mom's famous cookies.

"Michael, you can't eat all those cookies today," Yuna admonished.

"Aw man."

Leo had scrambled out of the armchair and was now sitting in front of Michael, eyeing the bag of cookies. Without any hesitation, Harper launched herself into the chair and settled in.

"Ah, the power of Dayo's cookies." She smirked to herself as Leo began pleading with Michael for a few.

After a few minutes, Kelly came running down again.

"I'm off to work," she said. "Sofia's out front."

Looking up, Harper could see Kelly was all made up and wearing her black puffy coat, making her look like some big bowling ball.

Yuna frowned. "What time are you going to be home?"

"Me and the girls are going to get a bite to eat after work, but I won't be too late!"

"You have school tomorrow," her mom responded.

"I know." Kelly rolled her eyes as she left the house.

Harper peered out the window where a little silver

car sat with Kelly's friend Sofia in the driver's seat. Sofia had helped Kelly get a job at a new makeup shop called Jeune, which had opened on Wisconsin Avenue. It was a standalone Victorian-style house painted a dark purple with black accents. It was kind of weird and funky, especially on a street that was mostly cute little cafés and shops. Lately, Kelly was almost always working there. Yuna was concerned because she wanted Kelly to focus on her schoolwork. Junior year was supposed to be the hardest year of high school. But it had been their dad who'd insisted that this job was good for Kelly.

Harper wasn't so sure. Kelly had become obsessed with cosmetics recently. When she wasn't working, she was reading fashion magazines and watching beauty tutorial videos. Kelly would put so much stuff on her face that at times she no longer looked like a seventeen-year-old high school student but someone much older. In fact, Harper was sure all the products Kelly was using were bad for her. Without makeup, her bare face looked unhealthy, something Harper was pretty sure shouldn't be happening. But how could she tell Kelly that her makeup was aging her?

THE BULLIES

A t school, Harper stifled a yawn as she moved with the flow of students filing through the seventh-grade hallway.

"Wake up, sleepy." A finger poked her in the side, and Harper turned to smile at her best friend, Dayo. She wore her medium-length brown hair like a thick cloud of curls that framed her pretty face and deep dimples.

Harper threw her arm around Dayo's shoulders, and the friends headed into the cafeteria, where they joined a table in the far-right corner of the room. Dayo had introduced Harper to her school friends on the first day, and they had all gotten along really well, although it was still hard for Harper to feel close to anyone outside of Dayo. There was Judy Chen, who was Chinese American and possibly the funniest person Harper had ever met. And Judy was best friends with Maya Giles, who was half-Black and half-white and quite possibly the prettiest girl in the whole school. And Maya was also the reason that Devon Marcus would sometimes sit at their table. Devon was definitely one of the cool athletic kids at school. He was tall with a medium-brown skin tone and styled his hair in a short fade with a faux-hawk up top that made him look super stylish. Harper would have been intimidated by him if he wasn't such a nice guy. And if he didn't clearly like Maya. He even made his not-as-nice friends treat Harper with respect. Also at their table regularly was Tyler Mercado, who was Filipino American and had dark hair with platinum-blond tips that he always spiked up, and Gabby Diaz, who proudly claimed her Mexican heritage and loved everything Korean. Tyler and Gabby were huge K-drama and K-pop fans and loved to talk about Korean things with Harper. Even though Dayo's cookies were always the star snack item, Harper made it a habit to bring a bag of Korean treats once a week just so she could hear Tyler and Gabby shriek in delight. At the end of their table were some other old friends of Dayo's who weren't as friendly to Harper, so she tended to avoid them.

As she sat down with Dayo, Tyler leaned over to tap her arm.

"Hey, Harper, I heard your cousin got jumped by Joey Ramos during gym today. Saw him at the nurse's office last period," he said. "His nose was bleeding bad."

"Crap!" Harper jumped to her feet, but Dayo pulled her back down.

"He's probably not there anymore," Dayo said.

Nodding, Harper pulled out her phone and texted Leo. **R U ok?**

"He's in class now," Dayo reminded her. "Eighth graders have lunch after us."

"Do you know what happened?" Harper asked.

Tyler shook his head. "Joey is bad news."

This was terrible. Leo had only been at Little Ridge Middle School for two weeks. Coming mid-semester in eighth grade was definitely not easy. But Harper had hoped Leo would avoid the notice of the wrong kids. Harper and Dayo exchanged uneasy glances. It looked like Leo was going to have a difficult year.

When school ended, Harper and Dayo waited by

the bike racks for Leo to come out. It had only been a few minutes when they saw his scrunched-up form and mousy-brown hair. A group of boys was walking behind—one minute Leo was heading toward them, the next he was facedown on the ground. The boys laughed as they surged past.

Harper and Dayo raced over to help him up.

"Leo, are you okay?"

They could immediately see the bruises covering his normally pale face.

Fists clenched at her sides, Harper glared at the group of boys, who was still glancing back and laughing. One boy sneered at her.

"What are you looking at?"

"Trash," Harper replied as she stared directly into his eyes.

The boy swore and made to approach her, but his friends grabbed him. "Come on, Joey, the bus is here."

"Harper." Dayo urged Harper away. "Let's go."

Leo was already on his bike and riding away as fast as he could. Dayo and Harper followed behind until they reached Dayo's house.

"I'm worried about Leo," Dayo said. "They're going to make his life miserable."

"Yeah, and he's already having a hard time because of the divorce," Harper said. "I know it must be hurting him, but he won't talk about it."

"Poor Leo," Dayo sighed. "I would cry every day if my parents divorced."

"Me too," Harper agreed. "I can't even imagine it."

Dayo clenched her right hand into a fist and shook it angrily. "Oh, that Joey Ramos is the worst!"

They looked at each other helplessly. What could they do when they were up against eighth graders? The only thing Harper could think of was to tell her parents.

At home, Harper put her bike in the garage and walked through the house to the study, where Leo was now staying. She knocked on the door for what felt like several minutes until he finally opened it.

"What?"

Harper gazed at his bruised face. "You've got to tell my parents."

"No way! That would be the biggest mistake. Then he'll get suspended or expelled, and his friends will never leave me alone."

Leo sat down and stretched out on his bed.

"So what are you gonna do?" Harper asked. "Just let him beat you up the rest of the year?"

"Look, if it gets to be too much for me, I'll force my parents to take me back and homeschool me," Leo responded. "At least the weather will be nice."

"That's true, I wasn't sure why you wanted to leave an island paradise for Washington, D.C., anyway."

He looked up at her in surprise. "I've always liked it here."

"You do?" Harper's eyes bugged out in surprise. "But why?"

"I like being with you guys," he replied. "It feels like family in a way that I never get with my parents. Like, at least you guys always get to eat dinner together. Well, most nights. I really hate eating by myself. And with the divorce, it's going to be worse."

Harper sat down next to her cousin on his bed and realized how lonely Leo was as an only child whose parents were constantly working and moving around.

"You know Michael. He'll never let you eat by yourself," Harper teased.

Leo laughed. "I kind of wish I had a little brother like Michael," he said wistfully. "I wouldn't mind being home alone so much."

"Well, there's plenty of him to go around while

you're here," she replied. "I'm going to take advantage of the quiet while he's at tae kwon do."

During dinner, Leo made light of his bruises as basketball injuries. Harper wasn't quite sure her parents bought it, but everyone was entertained by Michael's story about breaking his first board in tae kwon do class.

"I really didn't want to break the board, Harper," he was explaining. "I don't like to break things even when they tolded me to. It's not nice. Kelly hates it when I breakeded her things, and that was an accident."

Harper snickered at Kelly's sour face. Kelly had recently bought a whole bunch of makeup and skin care products and left them on the coffee table to show their mom. Michael had been playing tag with Leo and crashed into the table, knocking over all the bottles and jars and leaving a huge perfumed mess.

"So what happened, Michael?" Harper asked.

"Well, they said I have to break it to get my yellow belt, so I pretended it was that scary monster from the bad trees and I breakeded it!"

Everyone at the table got immediately tense. It was a reminder of the frightening situation they'd all been through during their holiday vacation on Razu Island.

"Good job, little buddy!" Harper gave Michael a high five, which he slapped enthusiastically. As he continued his story, Harper eyed the rest of her family, taking in the various degrees of discomfort. Her mom and dad were not a surprise. They never liked to talk about spiritual stuff. Leo was still shaken up by what had happened on the island. But Kelly was an enigma. Kelly had been with Harper when the monsters had come out of the tree. She was the only one who experienced what Harper and Dayo had gone through. Even Michael hadn't actually seen the real monsters; he'd only dreamed of them. But for some reason Kelly still refused to believe that anything terrible had happened on the island. It was as if she'd erased all the bad stuff.

Maybe it was a good thing, Harper thought. Perhaps it helped her sister sleep at night. Harper still dreamed of the Razu, hideous soul eaters who'd been trapped in the spiritual realm for centuries. But they'd coerced the Bennington Hotel family to help them collect souls in order to escape and walk the earth again. Had it not been for Harper and Dayo, their plan would have worked. It scared Harper to think of what would have happened if they hadn't been on the island at that exact time. When she'd asked her grandmother about it, Grandma had reassured her.

"Harper, as much as it feels like the weight of the world might have been on your shoulders, that is not true. Had the Razu escaped, there would have been others who would have stopped them. You are not alone," Grandma Lee had said. "There are people with powers like you who are protecting all of us."

Harper had felt a tremendous relief to hear her grandmother's words. She hadn't realized how oppressive the burden had been, feeling as if the fate of the world had rested on her and Dayo's shoulders.

Harper wondered what her life would be like if she never saw ghosts. She looked at her little brother still animatedly chatting away, and she knew she'd never give up her abilities, especially because of him. Michael had been the one targeted by evil ghosts when they'd first moved into their house and also on Razu Island. Had it not been for her abilities, she could have lost her brother forever. Harper had promised that she would always be there for him. She would keep him safe no matter what evil creatures were out there.

THE TRUE HISTORY OF MRS. DEVEREUX

"Grandma! How are you? Can you walk yet?"

Harper was so happy to hear her Grandma Lee laughing on the phone.

"Of course I can walk! How do you think I go to the bathroom? I'm not that old!"

"But you can't go out yet, right?"

Her grandmother sighed. "Doctor said I still have to be careful. But I'm getting better, Harper! Don't worry."

Slumping down in her seat, Harper frowned in dismay. "I guess I was hoping for a miracle so you could come home already."

"I'll see you soon enough," her grandma soothed.

"But in the meantime, why haven't you called Madame Devereux, like I asked you to?"

This was a question Harper was dreading.

"It's just that I've been so busy with schoolwork."

"Uh-huh." Grandma paused for a long moment. "Listen to me, Harper, this is very important. You must stop putting off the madame. If I was there, I'd be meeting with you every night!"

"And I'd do it with you, Grandma," Harper responded. "It's just that Mrs. Devereux scares me. I don't like calling her if I don't have to."

"My dearest girl, you have no choice. You must meet with her immediately," her grandmother said. "What you did on that island was amazing. You channeled pure spiritual energy directly. That is the most powerful thing in the world. But if you don't learn how to protect yourself, that power can become a destructive force."

"Grandma, I'm not going to turn bad."

"No child, you would never," her grandmother cut in. "But if an evil entity were to get control over you, do you know how to protect yourself?"

Harper had no response. If a ghost or a demon took control of her body, what could she do?

"That's what Madame Devereux will teach you,

Harper. To learn how to control your powers and protect yourself."

As much as she didn't want to, Harper knew she'd have to call the spiritual adviser.

"Okay, Grandma, I'll talk to her tonight."

After ending her call, Harper put a "Do Not Disturb" sign on the outside of her door and locked it. It was more to keep Michael from barging in, but it also helped keep her mom out during her sessions. Her mother didn't like any of the shaman rituals Harper had learned from her grandma.

She set out her bowls, her bottle of holy water, and her bells. Since she had gotten home from the island, she didn't need to sit in a circle of salt. Her grandmother had already placed enough protections around her house to keep it safe from spiritual attack. And Harper's first encounters with ghosts in their house had helped clear her home of all spirits. Although that didn't keep Harper from avoiding the basement. The memories still creeped her out.

Harper sat on the floor and placed the three bowls in front of her. She lit a match and set a white piece of paper on fire and caught the embers in her hand before dropping them in the first bowl. Filling the other two bowls with holy water, Harper closed her eyes and focused her thoughts on opening a channel with the spiritual world.

Immediately, a rich, beautiful voice filled the room.

"Took you long enough, Harper."

Harper opened her eyes to see Mrs. Devereux in a stunning red dress and an enormous matching hat covered in roses.

Harper blinked in surprise. "Wow! I've never seen you wear that before."

"I broke it out just for you," she said with a toothy smile. "Red is a power color, don't you think?"

"How are you able to change your clothes?"

"It's just an illusion, dearest," Mrs. Devereux said as she flickered through several outfits before returning to the crimson dress. "I present myself in the memories of my past self. Fortunately, I had a glorious wardrobe."

The ghost looked at the bowls of holy water and arched an elegant brow. "Harper, are you intending to trap me?"

"No, I was summoning you."

Mrs. Devereux let out a rich laugh. "You have so much to learn, little one. The purification ritual, your bells, and a ring of salt, which you forgot, are for when you must protect yourself. Like when you were at Razu Island. But your house is already well protected by your grandmother. All you have to do is summon me."

"Oh, I see."

"Now, let's not waste any more time," she said. She sat down on Harper's bed without making any depression on the mattress. "Let's see just how much you can do. I would take you to Woodlawn Cemetery to meet some of my friends, but it is far from here, and your mother would not like you out so late at night."

Harper nodded her head vigorously. Her mother would *definitely* not like it. She hated it when Harper went to cemeteries.

Mrs. Devereux pulled a beaded bag from behind her elbow and opened it in her lap.

Curious, Harper pointed at the bag. "You can actually hold things in it?"

"No, child, but I have always liked appearances, so humor me."

Slightly chastened by her tone, Harper sat back and watched as Mrs. Devereux pulled out three small items and placed them on the bed. A large diamond ring, a jeweled dagger, and a tiny crystal vial. It took a moment for Harper to realize they weren't real, but illusions.

"These were once my treasured items," Mrs. Devereux said. "If they were real, you would be able to get a stronger reading, but let's see what you can do with these memories."

Harper looked over the items that glowed with an otherworldly air and hesitated. How could she read what she couldn't touch?

"Harper, you don't need to feel something to be able to read it."

Not quite sure what Mrs. Devereux meant by that, Harper stared closer at the items. She was so used to touching something and having it trigger a vision that the idea of just looking at something seemed impossible. Especially when it was a memory of a memory. What could she even glean from it? As she stared at the items, a flash of light hit her eye, and something flew by quickly in her mind.

"Wait, what was that?" she whispered.

She looked for the flash of light again, and this time she zoned in on something. It was a gloved hand and it was holding the jeweled dagger. She watched as the hand used the dagger to cut and peel a persimmon.

"You cut fruit with your gloves on?"

Mrs. Devereux smiled. "I don't like getting my hands dirty. What kind of fruit did you see?"

"Persimmon," Harper replied.

"My favorite," Mrs. Devereux replied. "Good job. Can you see anything from the other two items?"

With a deep breath in and out, Harper focused on the ring. This time she heard a sound. Low laughter and heavy breathing.

"I see the ring on a hand. I hear laughing and, ew, kissing sounds."

Mrs. Devereux sat straight up and waved a hand over the ring, causing it to vanish.

"That was not the memory I thought you'd pick up on, young lady." Her eyes gleamed, and the corner of her mouth quivered as if she was holding back a laugh. "Now I'm very interested to see what you pick up from the vial."

There was something different about the vial. It was beautiful and had a drop of white fluid at the base. Harper detected something that looked like fumes emanating from it. She blinked, and she saw the hand with the ring holding the vial, sitting at an opulent desk. The person spun around to face large glass doors leading to a balcony, looking out over a dark, cloudy evening sky. A loud banging, and a frightened young face kneeling at the figure's feet. "They're coming for you, Madame!"

From the reflections of the windows, Harper

could see soldiers barging in through the door, rifles with bayonets pointed at the figure in the chair.

"Madame Devereux, you are wanted for murder!"

Harper watched the hand holding the crystal vial that was filled with a clear liquid. With one fluid motion, the figure brought the vial to her lips.

"Stop her, we must take her alive!"

The graceful hand dropped as the figure convulsed, and the vial rolled under the desk.

Horrified, Harper looked up at Mrs. Devereux with tears in her eyes. "You took poison! But why?"

Mrs. Devereux's beautiful brown eyes turned sorrowful. "I had no choice. They were performing vivisections on witches back then."

"Vivisections?"

"It's when they perform surgery on you while you are awake. You can feel everything they are doing to you."

Harper gasped. "That's torture!"

"They would have done that and far worse."

"I'm so sorry, ma'am." Harper impulsively tried to hug the ghost, causing Mrs. Devereux to chuckle.

"It's all right, dear one. It was a very long time ago. But now we must focus on you," she reminded Harper. "Today you are going to learn how to close your mind."

Wiping away her tears, Harper focused on the spirit's words.

"It's not that hard, especially for you," Mrs. Devereux continued. "You've done it several times already. Remember, on the island? I told you to hide your aura, and you hid from those soul eaters, the Razu."

Thinking back to that night, Harper remembered that she'd thought of Rose, her oldest friend. The ghost girl in the mirror who'd saved Harper when she was four years old and had become her best friend. Rose was gone now. She'd finally followed the light to where she belonged. But Harper missed her deeply. All she had were her memories. That's what she'd done. She'd lost herself in her memories of Rose, just like that child ghost Holly had done on Razu Island. Holly was the little girl who had been killed by the Razu many years ago. When Harper had asked Holly how she hid from the soul eaters, Holly had guided her. She had said, *I tried not to be afraid, even though they feel so scary. I think of my mommy and daddy and puppies and kittens. I flood my thoughts with things I love until the monsters go away.*

Thinking of Rose must have been how Harper had hidden herself also. When she explained it to Mrs. Devereux, the spiritual adviser clapped her hands in delight, although there was no clapping sound at all.

"Ah, Harper! You've discovered the power of love," she said. "There is nothing greater in the world."

Harper couldn't help herself from rolling her eyes.

"Excuse me, did you just roll your eyes at me, young lady?"

Chagrined, Harper hung her head. "Sorry, ma'am. It's just that I didn't expect you to say something so cheesy. You're, like, the coolest person I know in the whole entire world."

"Harper, love is not cheesy. It is the most powerful emotion. People kill for it. People will sacrifice themselves for it. It can both heal you and destroy you. There is no greater power, and you should not underestimate it."

"Yes, ma'am."

"Good, now dim your aura for me."

Taking a deep breath, Harper closed her eyes and let her mind take her back to the meadow with Rose. Once again, she could smell the crispness of the air and mist. In the distance, a girl with bright red hair was walking toward her, smiling and waving in delight. It was Rose! Harper threw open her arms and raced toward her friend . . .

"Excellent! Your aura completely disappeared! It

was as if you weren't even here anymore!"

Discombobulated, Harper blinked in surprise to see Mrs. Devereux's intense expression.

"Tell me, Harper, where were you?"

"I'm not sure," Harper responded in amazement. "It's a meadow that Rose was in, but I don't think I've ever been there in real life."

"Fascinating," Mrs. Devereux said. "You went into a memory that was not yours. It was probably Rose's. How did you know to go there?"

"I really don't know." Harper twirled her hair as she tried to figure out how she knew of the place. "To be honest, it was like it called to me. I was looking for Rose, and this place told me she was there. That's why I went."

The spiritual adviser was quiet for a long moment. "Let's try something else," she mused aloud. "Harper, this time instead of Rose, think of your grandma."

With a resolute nod, Harper closed her eyes and pictured her grandma as she'd seen her last. In bed at her aunt's house in Queens, New York. As she focused in on the memory, she could suddenly hear Monty barking, as if he were in the room with her. Harper focused on the walls first. The bright yellow color of Aunt Youjin's guest room. Suddenly, Harper was right there, and her grandma was staring back at her in absolute shock!

"Grandma!" Harper beamed in delight.

"Harper! How did you get here?"

Before she could answer, her grandma's door opened and her aunt Youjin showed up, holding her new baby.

"Time to visit your grandma," she said as she walked right through Harper's ghostly form.

"Hey!" Harper said. But the next minute, she was whisked out of the room again. When she opened her eyes, Mrs. Devereux was staring intently at her.

"Aw man, I was just saying hi to Grandma!"

For the very first time, it was clear that Harper had shocked the spirit. Her expression was one of complete and utter disbelief.

"Remarkable, Harper. Simply remarkable. You projected yourself through the astral plane to another location," Mrs. Devereux said. "You spirit traveled. And yet you are not a spirit."

"Oh, so that's why my aunt didn't see me!" Harper realized. "She even walked right through me! That was so weird."

Mrs. Devereux stood absolutely still before folding her hands across her stomach.

"This is a huge development. I must talk to Madam

about this immediately." And without another word, the spirit disappeared.

"Sheesh, I wish I could have talked to Grandma a little longer," Harper muttered to herself. "Oh, hey! I can go back now!"

Just as she was about to project herself again, Mrs. Devereux poofed back, right in front of her face, causing Harper to reel back in shock.

"Gah! Ma'am, you scared me!"

"I know what you are thinking, Harper girl, but don't do it." Mrs. Devereux wagged a finger at her. "Do not enter the astral plane alone, it is too dangerous. You could get lost there and invite danger to your physical body."

"But—"

"Don't test my patience." Mrs. Devereux's entire presence seemed to grow larger, frightening Harper.

"Yes, ma'am."

As soon as she left, Harper collapsed onto her bed, clenching her chest.

"She's so scary," she whimpered to herself.

LESSONS WITH
MRS. DEVEREUX

In the morning, Harper and Leo rode their bikes to Dayo's house first, and they all headed to school together. The weather had gotten blustery cold, and their faces were frozen by the time they locked up their bikes in front of the building. Leo took off into the building, not bothering to wait for the girls.

"Jeez, not even a good-bye," Harper huffed.

"I don't blame him," Dayo said. "He's probably trying to get inside before Joey and his crew show up."

"Oh, right." Harper sighed. "We gotta figure out a way to help him."

"Too bad we can't haunt him," Dayo said. "If anyone deserved it, it would be Joey."

Struck by Dayo's words, Harper froze in midstep. If Rose was still with them, she would definitely have helped out. Especially because it was Harper and Rose's prank that had caused Leo to start seeing ghosts. Rose had always felt guilty about scaring Leo. But without her ghost friend, how could they haunt anyone?

Not recognizing Harper's thinking face, Dayo grabbed Harper by the arm and pulled her into the building.

The rest of the day, Harper plotted and schemed and wondered how she could pull off a haunting.

"There's no way Mrs. Devereux would do anything like this," Harper said to Dayo as they walked their bikes home, in deep conversation. "And we just don't know any nice ghosts anymore."

"Even if we did, I'm not sure it's a good idea, Harper," Dayo said.

"But it was your idea!"

"Yeah, but even Rose didn't like that haunting prank you pulled on Leo," Dayo reminded her.

"But this is different. Joey is a real bad guy."

"Still, asking a ghost to scare a human just seems wrong," Dayo said. "But if we pretended to be ghosts and scared him ourselves, that would be different."

Harper froze in thought again. Why couldn't she

pretend to be a ghost? She smiled in anticipation.

"Don't do that. You're scaring me," Dayo remarked.

"I have an idea."

"The answer is no," Dayo stated.

"But you haven't even heard it yet!"

Dayo gave Harper a suspicious side-eye. "I don't trust your smile."

"What? You can trust me!"

Walking away, Dayo shook her head. "I got a bad feeling."

Running to catch up with her friend, Harper hurriedly told her the plan. Harper would haunt Joey on Friday night and scare him witless, to warn him against bullying Leo. Harper told Dayo about traveling the astral plane. All she would need was something of Joey's to guide her to him.

Dayo stopped walking and gazed unblinkingly at her friend.

"Astrology what?"

"Astral plane. It's how spirits move between the spiritual world and ours," Harper responded.

"But how can you . . . ?" Dayo blinked rapidly. "You're not a ghost."

"I know it's hard to believe. I even shocked Mrs. Devereux when I did it, and you know she's never surprised by anything. Apparently, I can project my soul through the astral plane while my body stays in the physical world," Harper explained. "Which is why Mrs. D told me not to do it alone. Because it's dangerous."

"Dangerous! How?"

"Something about inviting danger to my body."

"Then this is definitely an absolutely terrible idea, Harper!" Dayo's pretty brown eyes almost bugged out in alarm.

"No, hear me out! It's brilliant!"

Harper pleaded with Dayo all the way home, but Dayo wouldn't budge. She refused to do anything that would put Harper in danger.

But what else could they do to help Leo? Harper couldn't let Leo continue to be bullied. He was having a hard enough time already. While there was nothing she could do about the divorce, she could stop Joey from bothering Leo. She knew she could. She just had to convince Dayo to help her.

That night, Grandma FaceTimed Harper to talk about the projection experience.

"Harper, you gave me such a scare when you showed up like that, without any warning," her grandma chided.

"I'm sorry, Grandma, but Mrs. Devereux told me to think of you!"

"I'm pretty sure you were supposed to think of a memory of me, not the real me!"

"Yeah, she was definitely surprised. Was it so bad?"

"No, honey, it was great! But it is a huge power, and you have to protect yourself before you do that again."

"Protect myself from what? I didn't understand what Mrs. Devereux was saying."

Grandma Lee looked very concerned.

"Harper, when you leave your body to enter the astral plane, you open yourself up to two very different dangers. The first are the unknown dangers already hiding in the astral plane. If you get lost or separated from your body for too long, you might never return."

"Okay, that's terrifying."

"The second danger is what you might invite back into your body because it is open to the astral plane. You don't know what entity could find its way to your body and possess you. This is why you must never do that alone! You cannot leave your body unprotected. Promise me, Harper."

"I promise, Grandma."

"Good. Now get ready for another lesson with Mrs. Devereux tonight. She will teach you how to protect yourself in the astral plane."

After hanging up with her grandma, Harper prepared to invite Mrs. Devereux into her room again. Soon the spirit arrived, this time dressed in a purple gown that was almost black. As always, Mrs. Devereux looked gorgeous.

"So tonight, Madam wants me to teach you how to protect yourself in the astral plane. Even though you've already agreed not to go there alone, am I right?" Mrs. Devereux gave Harper a knowing look.

"Yes, ma'am."

"But we also know that knowledge is power. So, we are going to teach you how to stay safe."

That's exactly what Harper needed.

"What you are going to do, Harper, is to remember that you are not supposed to be in the astral plane, because you are not of the astral plane. Therefore, you must not attract any attention to yourself. You have to be stealthy. You don't make a scene, and you don't let your presence be felt."

"How do I do that?"

"You stick to the reason you are there in the first place. In and out. You don't go wandering. That's where the danger's at. Once you are off course, it's easy to get lost. Because it is an infinite space. It doesn't work like physical space here, as you know it."

Harper didn't understand what Mrs. Devereux meant.

"How is it different?"

"Think of it this way. When a spirit is in the physical world, it doesn't abide by physical constraints. It can move through solid things. That's how the astral plane works. There are no physical limitations. It is space and time with no road maps. You are using the astral plane to shortcut the physical world. So, you must always enter the plane with a specific destination in mind, and you must always come right back to your body. As long as you remember that, you should be safe."

Harper nodded. That was easy enough.

"But if you run into something you shouldn't, then you must remember not to talk to it. Show no emotion, especially not fear. Don't tell it anything about you. And whatever you do, you must not lead it back to your body."

A shudder coursed through Harper.

"What's out there, ma'am?"

"Something wicked," Mrs. Devereux replied. "And truly evil."

* * *

The next several nights, Harper trained with Mrs. Devereux to learn how to hide her aura and how to protect herself from those who would possess her.

"Remember, child, your strength is inside of you. It is your mind—it is not only your defense, but your weapon. If I try to force myself on you, you must use all your willpower to turn me away. Do not let me in. Raise a shield, like an iron wall. Stop me. Can you do that, child?"

Mrs. Devereux tried to enter Harper's mind. It felt like a sharp push against her head. Harper imagined a fortress around her head, strong and tall and impenetrable. Immediately, the pushing stopped.

"Good. Now, stopping me is not enough. You must fight me off. You must defeat me. You must send me out of the physical plane."

Harper held up her hands helplessly. She had no idea what to do.

"Harper, when you went to your grandmother's house for the first time this past summer, do you remember what I said to you about your powers?"

Searching back in her memories, Harper envisioned her grandmother's house and meeting Mrs. Devereux. Harper had asked the spirit adviser how she knew that Harper had the power to become a spirit hunter.

"Because I felt your power," Mrs. Devereux had said. *"You summoned an entire cemetery of ghosts. You willed them to help you, and then you summoned me. That is the act of a powerful spirit hunter. You must channel your spiritual energy, the pure force within you that allows you to see us."*

"Yes, and you said that was why I could use the bells to fight evil," Harper remembered. "But how can I fight without my bells?"

"Think, Harper. What do your bells do?"

"They disrupt? They bind?"

"Yes, now use your mind to do the same thing."

Harper just stared at Mrs. Devereux blindly. "I don't understand."

"Use the power of your mind like your bells. Attack, disrupt, bind, release."

Blinking in confusion, Harper thought about her bells and her chants. She thought of what her grandmother had taught her.

"These bells are based on Buddhist principles of wisdom and truth." The Wisdom bell had a bright medium sound that was crystal clear, while the Truth bell sounded lower and deeper in tone. *"Wisdom opens the spiritual pathways, for knowledge is power. Truth reveals what is hidden, for a spirit cannot hide from the sound of truth. The sound of these bells is anathema to an evil spirit— it will immobilize them when used with the proper words.*

38

When you ring the bell of Wisdom you must say, 'Through the power of the Ancient One, I bind you. You will do no harm.' When you ring the bell of Truth you must say, 'Through the power of the Worthy One, I bind you. You will do no harm.'"

"Am I supposed to chant?" Harper asked hesitantly.

The spirit guide seemed to flicker in annoyance. The next minute, Harper was floating in the air.

"What are you doing?"

"I have no physical form, and yet how am I lifting you?"

Shaking her head, Harper said, "I don't know."

"Yes, you do. Remember what I told you."

"Through spiritual energy?"

"Yes, and what did your grandmama tell you to do with that spiritual energy?"

"Harness it into a power source," Harper replied as Mrs. Devereux set her gently onto her feet. "But how?"

"That you must figure out for yourself. But remember, there are no limits to what your mind can do. You can fight back!"

Frustrated, Harper shook her head. "It would be better if I could make my bells come to me!"

"Then do it," Mrs. Devereux said.

"How?"

"Why are you asking me, child? Use your brain!"

Harper threw her hands up in exasperation. "But I don't know what to do!"

"So, you're just going to give up, then? Just like that?"

"No, I just need help . . ."

"What do you think I'm doing? You think I like wasting my time hanging around with you when all you can say is 'I don't know'?"

Closing her eyes, Harper took a deep breath. "Just tell me what to do."

"I can't tell you how to use your own head!" Mrs. Devereux gave the most eloquent and yet exasperated shrug, that had Harper ready to rip her own hair out.

"But you're the expert!" Harper said through clenched teeth.

"Harper Raine! You're the only one who knows how to do what you can do!"

"You're not listening to me."

"*You* are not listening to me," Mrs. Devereux retorted.

"But I don't know what to do!"

"Yes, you do! Stop questioning me and just do it!" the spiritual adviser shouted, her voice echoing like thunder.

Furious, Harper slammed her hands on the floor and screamed, "Give me my bells!"

A sudden cacophony of jangling bells could be heard from the closet. Then suddenly the closet door flew open, and Harper's bells appeared before her.

Harper's jaw dropped open as she blinked furiously at the sight before her.

Mrs. Devereux smirked. "I told you you could do it."

Harper was still stunned. "But how?"

"Do you remember what you felt and thought?"

"I was angry and wanted my bells. So, I thought, *Give them to me now . . .*"

"And you forced them to come to you," Mrs. Devereux responded. "Think about how you did that, and practice some more."

Someone was knocking on her door.

"Harper, are you all right? Can you open the door, honey?"

The spiritual adviser floated above Harper and stretched luxuriously. It amazed Harper how everything Mrs. Devereux did, even something as mundane as stretching, could look so smooth and graceful.

"You'd better let your mother in," Mrs. Devereux said. "I'm tired and deserve a small break. We shall continue again in three days' time."

"Yes, ma'am, and thank you."

The spiritual adviser smiled at Harper. "You will be a very powerful spirit hunter, child. I see it in you."

And with that she vanished.

HARPER TEACHES THE BULLY A LESSON

Friday afternoon

The last-period bell rang, and Harper raced over to the eighth-grade wing to watch for Leo. Soon she saw her cousin heading out, closely followed by Joey and his friends. Once outside, they circled him.

"Yo, new kid," Joey said, shoving Leo. "Where you off to? We just wanna talk to you."

His friends started cracking up as they moved in tighter.

"I don't want any trouble," Leo responded.

"I don't care," Joey sneered.

Livid, Harper ran straight into the boy's back, shouting, "Move, people! Get out of my way!" Shoving him hard to the ground, Harper then deliberately smashed herself into the other boys, knocking them all down like dominoes, even Leo. She then ran as fast as she could toward the bicycle racks. As planned, Dayo, Judy, Maya, Tyler, and Gabby were all waiting in front of the school.

At lunch earlier, it had been Tyler who'd informed Harper that he overheard Joey saying he'd be "talking" to Leo after school. Everyone knew what kind of conversation this would be. Dayo wanted to report the bullies to the school administration, but Harper had a better idea. She needed something of Joey's (that part only Dayo knew about), and she also needed to divert his attention from Leo (this part needed all her friends' help). When the group had heard Harper's plan to draw Joey away from Leo, they all thought it was a terrible idea. And yet everyone, except for Devon (who had soccer practice), was there to help. A rush of gratitude sent adrenaline kicking through her veins. Harper bolted over to her friends and jumped onto her bike, which Dayo had unlocked beforehand. In seconds, Harper was on her bike and pedaling away. Sneaking a peek over her shoulder, Harper could see that her friends had executed the second part of her plan perfectly. They were just supposed to get in the bullies' way enough to give Harper a good head start. Maya and Judy had excitedly bumped into Joey while Tyler, Gabby, and Dayo deliberately stepped into the path of the other boys.

She could hear the shouts as the boys chased her, but she led them the wrong way and then rode her bike too fast for them to catch up. After ten minutes of running the bullies around, she headed home. She couldn't wait to try out her newfound skills on that rotten Joey Ramos. Harper had been practicing all night, moving things around her room. Once she realized that the very air around her was filled with energy, she could envision floating certain objects and making them come to her. She was excited to show Dayo what she could do.

She found Dayo and Leo waiting out front.

"Harper! Are you okay? I was so worried they'd catch you!"

Harper grinned. "They never had a chance."

Leo shook his head, looking both angry and worried.

"Harper, that was not smart! Those boys are going to come after you on Monday!"

Harper shrugged. "Unlike you, Leo, I have no problem telling my parents about those jerks. And I would enjoy watching my mom make a huge stink."

At her words, Leo became visibly angry. "Stay out of my business, Harper. I don't want your parents involved!"

"But why? They would make sure he can't bully you anymore," Harper said.

"I don't want to bother them."

"They would want to know about this, Leo."

"I said no!" Leo shouted. "Because they'd tell my parents and they'd insist on talking to me about it and then they'd blame each other and start fighting again. And I just can't deal with it. I can't deal with them!"

With one last glare at both Harper and Dayo, Leo stormed inside.

Dayo waited until he closed the door. "Maybe you should listen to him," she said.

Harper shook her head. "No, this is more reason than ever to do it my way. Without involving my parents."

Dayo grimaced. "Did you get what you needed?" she asked.

Harper nodded and pulled out one black glove. "I grabbed it out of his pocket just as he fell."

Dayo looked impressed. "Do you think it will work?"

Harper shrugged. "We'll find out tonight. When are you coming over?"

"Let me go get my bag, and I'll come in about an hour."

"Okay, great. Michael should be home from tae kwon do by then. He'll be happy to see you."

At dinner, Harper was surprised to find that her mother had cooked something for a change. Spaghetti with meat sauce, salad, and garlic bread. It was one of the few dishes she made well and made lots of. Which meant leftovers for the next day, but Harper didn't mind. It meant she could eat it instead of frozen pizza, which she despised. For dessert, her mother had bought a blueberry pie with vanilla ice cream. It wasn't as good as Dayo's mom's desserts, but it hit the spot.

"Hey, Aunt Yuna, that was pretty good!"

"Yes, Mrs. Raine, dinner was delicious!"

"Thank you, Dayo and Leo! This is such high praise coming from the two of you!"

"Mom, you're a great cook!" Harper said. "You just need to do it a little more often."

Yuna laughed. "Okay, Harper! I'll try!"

Harper could see how happy her mom was with the compliments and hoped it meant she would try to cook some more. Harper loved home-cooked meals the best, but her mom was always busy and her dad could only make breakfast foods. Maybe Dayo's mom's delicious cooking was rubbing off on Yuna.

After dinner, Dayo and Harper went up to the bedroom to prepare for the haunting.

"Okay, Harper, show me your skills," Dayo said excitedly.

Grinning, Harper sat cross-legged on the floor in front of Dayo and concentrated on pulling the sock off her friend's foot. Once it was off, Harper let it float around the room. As the sock soared over to Dayo's head, she covered her mouth and let out a muted scream. She rubbed her eyes, and then she slapped herself on her cheeks.

"Is this for real? Am I awake?"

In response, Harper sent the sock flying into Dayo's face. Dayo ducked and giggled.

"Oh my God! Harper, you're doing telekinesis! Like superhero stuff!"

The sock went swooping around the room.

"How are you doing that? I can't believe it!" Dayo said.

"I don't really know," Harper said. At that moment, the sock fell to the floor. "But it takes all my concentration, as you can see."

"So you have to think about it intensely to make it move?"

Tilting her head to the side, Harper tried to think about what she was doing. "Not thinking, more like moving the energy around it. Does that make sense?"

"Not really," Dayo laughed. "But whatever you say! Do you think you could move something bigger, like yourself?"

Taking a deep breath, Harper tried to levitate herself. But all she managed to do was stir up a slight breeze.

"I think I'll have to practice a lot more to get to that point."

"Okay, so how does the haunting work, then?" Dayo asked.

Pulling out the black glove, Harper placed it on the floor.

"This should lead me to him," she replied. "I'll go at midnight. And then, once I'm there, I'm going to scare the bloody hell out of him."

"What're you gonna do?"

"Oh, I'm just going to move things around . . ."

She gave Dayo an evil grin, but Dayo looked really nervous.

"But what if something bad happens? Didn't you

say your grandmother told you not to go there?"

"She said not to go alone. That's why you're here! You'll watch over me and pull me back if I take too long."

"I'm just worried about you."

"Don't be. I know what I'm doing," Harper reassured her. "I'm following Mrs. D's advice. I'll go in and out. Fifteen minutes tops. You have the timer, and if I'm not back in fifteen, you'll call me and wake me up."

"Why do I have a bad feeling about this?"

Harper ignored her own twinges of nerves and her guilty conscience. "It'll be all right," she said out loud. "Everything will be all right."

Neither girl could sleep, so they stayed awake watching funny animal videos until it was midnight. Taking a deep breath, Harper pulled out the glove and whispered, "Wish me luck."

Before she could go, Dayo stopped her. "Wait! Are you sure this is a good idea?"

For a moment, Harper hesitated, but she thought of Leo and hardened her resolve. There was so much fear and sadness in his eyes when he talked about his parents. Their divorce was incredibly hard on him. He didn't need any other burdens.

"I'm gonna make sure Joey leaves Leo alone from now on."

The two girls nodded at each other.

"You got your timer ready?" Harper asked.

Dayo showed the timer setting on her phone, set for fifteen minutes.

"As soon as the timer beeps, if I'm not back, you call my name and shake me hard to bring me back, okay?"

Looking very scared, Dayo nodded. "Please be careful, Harper."

"Don't worry. I will."

Focusing all her attention on the glove, Harper closed her eyes and let the memory of the glove's owner pull her out of her body and into the astral plane. The first thing she noticed was how dim it was, as if she were in a poorly lit tunnel. But something pulled her along quickly until suddenly she popped out into a bedroom. A lamp was on at the desk, and she could see Joey sitting in front of his computer, playing a game.

He wasn't asleep. Maybe that was even better, Harper thought. Turning her attention to the lamp, Harper focused her mind on unscrewing the light bulb until the room went dark.

"What the . . . ?" Joey got up and tried to turn the lamp on and off.

Harper then turned off the computer.

"What's going on?"

Taking note of a television on the other side of the room, Harper clicked it on and raised the volume up loud.

"What the heck is happening?!"

Joey jumped across the room to turn off the TV. He was looking completely freaked out.

Laughing to herself, Harper turned the computer back on and opened a Word document and began to type.

Joey is a bad boy. Joey is a bully. Joey will be punished.

She repeated her typing. Over and over again.

Joey was desperately trying to erase the words, but they kept typing no matter what he did.

Harper turned on the television again and raised the volume. Then, turning to the closet, she pulled out an outfit and let it move toward Joey slowly like a walking scarecrow, which turned out to be his breaking point. He began screaming and went flying out of his room.

Giggling madly, Harper willed herself out of the room and was swept into the dimness of the astral plane. But instead of being pulled rapidly toward a destination, she found herself floating in place.

Why wasn't she being pulled toward her body? Why was she stuck?

Harper forced herself to start moving, trying to figure out where to go. Looking for a clue. But all around her was a vast emptiness. She didn't understand where she was. No matter where she looked, there was nothing. No buildings. No streets. Nothing.

Desperate, she called out to Dayo, hoping she'd hear her.

"Dayo! Can you hear me?"

The silence stretched around her, suffocating her.

"Hello! Is anyone here?"

Harper felt the presence first. A heaviness in the air.

A voice answered her.

"Who are you? Or *what* are you?"

The voice was hoarse and menacing and absolutely terrifying.

Harper stared into a dark abyss of nothingness. The voice was coming from deep within, and suddenly, she spotted a pair of red pointed pupils gleaming at her.

Horrified, she suddenly remembered Mrs. Devereux's admonition. Don't speak. Don't respond.

"I asked, who are you? Are you human? Are you

spirit? You smell so delightful!"

Dragging her gaze away from the horror of the approaching voice, Harper tried to flee. She wanted to go anywhere, just as long as it was far from the frightening voice heading her way. A small but steady light appeared in the far distance. Hoping it was her way out, Harper began to float as fast as she could toward it.

"Where are you going? Come back! I'm so hungry."

Terrified by its words, Harper forced herself to move faster, but the heaviness of its presence was dragging her back.

"Harper, wake up!"

Dayo's voice sounded as if it was coming from far away, but Harper felt the immediate pull of it. It was coming from the light. From behind her, she could see the dark form getting closer. Frantic, Harper raced toward the ever-growing brightness.

"Come back, morseling." The voice whispered so close to her.

Harper tried not to scream, but she could feel it gaining on her.

"Harper, wake up now!"

Harper opened her eyes and saw Dayo's anxious face.

Bursting into tears, Harper hugged her friend tight.

"Are you all right? I was getting really worried!"

"Thank goodness you called me, Dayo! I was in trouble! You saved me!"

"What happened?"

"I don't know what it was, but something was chasing me through the astral plane," Harper whispered. "It was terrifying because I had no idea what it was. All I knew was that it was after me."

Dayo shuddered. "You're not allowed to do this again, Harper, I mean it!"

Harper nodded fervently. "I won't. I promise. I was really scared."

Harper was so freaked out that it took her a long time to fall asleep. But finally exhausted, she nodded off, only to find herself back in the astral plane in a nightmare where she couldn't move. The voice kept getting closer and closer.

A loud knocking on the door woke Harper from her nightmares.

"Who is it?" she called out groggily.

Kelly popped her head into the room. "Hey, you sleepyheads! I'm heading to work, but I wanted to tell you to come over at noon to the shop. We are giving away a free lip balm if you come in and sign up for our newsletter."

"Nope," Harper said as she pulled the covers over her head.

"Oh, I want one!" Dayo eagerly sat up on her air mattress next to Harper and nudged her. "Come on. Let's go, please?"

"Kelly, can't you just bring one home for Dayo?"

"No can do." Kelly shook her head. "One per customer, and it's a limited supply for today's event only. They come in really pretty colors, and the earlier you come, the better chance of choosing the color you want. So you should probably get there fifteen minutes early!"

"Thanks, Kelly. We'll definitely be there!" Dayo said enthusiastically.

Harper groaned loudly as Kelly left.

"Do we have to?"

Dayo grabbed her pillow, stood up, and hit Harper with it.

"After scaring me to death last night, the least you can do is something fun. Something absolutely not related to spirits and haunting." She punctuated every third word with a pillow punch.

"Okay! Okay! You win!"

Harper climbed out of bed and scratched her

head hard, causing Dayo to giggle.

"You look terrible."

Harper sighed. "I feel terrible. I had nightmares all night."

"About the astral plane?"

Harper nodded and shuddered. "That voice and those red eyes were all I could see."

Dayo reached over and grabbed Harper's hands. "Don't think about it anymore! You'll never see that monster thing again! It's going to be okay!"

Harper squeezed Dayo's hands, but in her heart, she wasn't so sure.

HOUSE OF JEUNE

Dayo and Harper rode their bikes to the makeup shop. It was farther down from where the mall was, making it a longer ride, but it was on a block that was a mix of houses and little cafés and shops. They locked their bikes on a rack in the middle of the block and walked over to Kelly's makeup store. The old Victorian-style house situated on the corner had a bright pink neon sign in the front bay windows that flashed "Jeune"—very obnoxiously. Harper hated it.

"Oh, it's so cool," Dayo sighed.

Harper gave her an incredulous look. "Are you serious?"

Beaming with excitement, Dayo grabbed Harper

by the hand and dragged her inside. At the door, a pretty sales clerk wearing a black uniform and way too much makeup pointed them to the back of the store. Weaving through the shelves filled with makeup, they reached an open space with counters and lots of chairs and what looked like a little stage. A line had formed of people with bags full of makeup they'd already bought. Another clerk came over and handed each of the girls a ticket with a number so that they would get a swag bag at the end of the presentation.

"I'm twenty-one and you're twenty-two," Dayo said. "We're gonna get some goodies for sure!"

"Presentation? What do they mean by that?" Harper asked.

"I think there's a makeup demonstration first," Dayo said.

A pretty young girl with long brown hair and glasses who was standing right next to them turned to agree.

"Yeah, it's going to be by Jenna. She's the owner of Jeune, which is why our moms brought us here." The girl pointed to two moms who were chatting with some salespeople about different makeup products. "They are big fans of hers and use all her products. We're just here because our moms promised to take

59

us to the movies afterward."

She gestured to two other younger girls, who looked bored, which Harper could totally relate to.

"I get it. The only reason we're here is because my sister works at this store and made us promise to come by," Harper said. And just at that moment, her sister appeared and made a beeline toward them. "Speak of the devil."

"Oh good, Harper, Dayo, you came! Do me a favor and give out these promo cards to everyone on the line, okay? Thanks!"

After shoving a stack of postcards into Harper's hands, Kelly sprinted to the back of the store again and disappeared.

Before she could say another word, the three girls crowded closer to her.

"Your name is Harper?" the younger girl with beautiful blond hair asked in surprise. "But that's my name, too!"

Harper blinked. "No way! I've never met someone who has the same name as me!"

"Me neither!" The other Harper grinned.

"Wow, that's so cool!" Laughing, they started grilling each other for information, and even discovered they had many more things in common.

"And what are your friends' names?" Dayo asked.

The girl with glasses introduced herself as Lia and her little sister, Kai. And as they chatted, they realized that Lia, the oldest, would be attending their middle school the following year.

"That's awesome! We'll be eighth graders by then and will definitely look out for you!" Dayo said.

"And you two will have to keep an eye out for my little brother, Michael," Harper said. "He's a kinder-gartner, but I know he would like you guys a lot!"

Little Harper and Kai smiled and nodded in agreement. Harper suddenly realized that the line had gotten really long.

"Argh, I guess I'd better give these out," she groused.

"We can help you," Lia said. "That way we can get it done quickly."

"Gee, thanks guys!" Harper divvied up the cards with the three girls, leaving Dayo to save their place in line. Harper, Lia, Kai, and Harper quickly gave away all the cards and got back in line just as the lights dimmed. Then one of the employees grabbed a microphone and began to introduce the event.

"Welcome to Jeune! We are so excited to have you at this premier event, where our founder, Jenna Gra-ham, will show you some makeup tricks and secrets. A few lucky guests will get a full makeover today!"

There were loud cheers from the audience, and a little spotlight came on as the spokesperson loudly introduced the owner. She came out from a curtained door behind the little stage. Jenna Graham was a very pale, very elegant woman who looked like she was in her late thirties or early forties. She had long wavy black hair and piercing green eyes. They were such an unusual green that Harper was sure they had to be contact lenses. But the thing that Harper noticed most sharply was that this smiling woman waving at the crowd had cold dead-fish eyes.

Leaning over toward Dayo, Harper whispered, "There's something about her that I really don't like."

Dayo nodded. "She gives me the creeps."

"Do we still have to stay here?"

"Yes. I'm not leaving until I get my lip balm!"

"Rats."

Jenna was charming the crowd, complimenting various women. She was wearing a very stylish ruby-red blouse and black pants that she paired with a beautiful black-and-white cameo necklace.

They watched as two overly excited young women got called up as volunteers. Two makeup artists began to do their makeup, while Jenna critiqued and gave step-by-step instructions to the audience. Harper was about ready to drop dead from boredom when she caught something weird in the reflection of the mirror. Each volunteer was positioned in front of a counter with a large mirror. Harper was sitting where she could see the front of one woman and the reflection in the mirror of the second. As the makeup artist applied foundation on the second woman's face, the reflection showed her skin sagging and wrinkling like an old person.

Incredulous, Harper blinked her eyes and stared at the reflection again. But now it appeared to be the smooth skin of a young person. What was it that she just saw happen?

This time she stared at the face of the woman in front of her. She watched carefully as the foundation was applied. To Harper, it looked as if the rich vibrant skin tone of the woman was being dulled and muted into a polished mannequin look. She didn't understand what was happening. They were hiding the woman's real color and covering it up with a fake one. The woman now looked older and less attractive, and yet everyone applauded as if she'd been changed into some beautiful model. Why couldn't they see what she was seeing? This makeup was not good for them. Yet Harper could hear the applause and the comments of the audience.

"Beautiful!"

"Gorgeous!"

The comments were all so positive. Harper didn't get it. Were her eyes deceiving her?

When the makeup artist was done, Jenna handed one woman a large antique silver hand mirror and told her to look at the "new you."

The woman's back was to Harper, and as she raised the mirror to her face, Harper caught the gleam of red eyes staring out at her from the woman's reflection. The same red eyes from the astral plane! They were fixated on her, watching her, as if to say "I've found you."

Harper gasped and shrank back in fright.

"What's the matter?" Dayo whispered.

"I have to go now," Harper muttered. Not waiting for Dayo, Harper stumbled to her feet and pushed her way through the onlookers to exit the store.

Out in the sunlight, Harper gasped for air and shivered in the frigid winter temperature. But she was grateful to be away from those chilling eyes.

"Harper, are you okay?" Dayo asked, patting her on the back.

"No, I'm not," Harper wheezed. "I saw it again. That demon or monster or whatever it was. I saw it in the reflection of the hand mirror. And it saw me."

Dayo's eyebrows were crinkled in alarm. "We have to tell your grandmother."

Harper shook her head vehemently. "No. Then Mrs. Devereux will find out and . . ." Harper shuddered. "She scares me."

"You have a choice, Harper: the demon monster or Mrs. Devereux."

"Hmmmmm . . ."

"Harper!"

"Okay, okay! I'll tell my grandma today."

Dayo put an arm around Harper's shoulders and guided her toward their bikes. "Let's at least go eat at the mall on our way home. I'm hungry."

Then Harper suddenly remembered the lip balm Dayo wanted. "Ah, Dayo, I'm sorry about the gift bags. Do you want to go back and I'll wait for you out here?"

Dayo shook her head. "Nah, I wasn't that impressed with their stuff anyway."

Surprised, Harper grabbed Dayo's hand. "Did you see their faces turn old?"

"Huh? What are you talking about?" Dayo asked in confusion.

"The makeup, it made them look old," Harper explained.

"Um, no," Dayo responded slowly. "I didn't see anything like that, I just thought the makeovers weren't that good."

"Exactly! That's because their stuff is terrible!" Harper agreed.

"Yeah, it was weird how the makeup didn't make them look better."

"Right? They looked worse. Like ugly trolls."

Sputtering, Dayo smacked Harper on the arm. "They weren't that bad!"

"Mm, okay, like old gnarly witches."

"Harper!"

"What?"

THE DEMON IN THE
ASTRAL PLANE

That night for dinner, her mother had ordered Lebanese food, which Harper loved. The platter on the table was filled with chicken shawarma and chicken kebab, hummus, baba ghanoush, spinach pies, falafel, stuffed grape leaves, salad, and pita bread. As she made herself a huge sandwich filled with all her favorite ingredients, she noticed her sister was barely eating. This surprised her, as Lebanese was most definitely one of Kelly's favorite meals.

Harper found herself studying her sister. Once again, Kelly was wearing a lot of makeup, and it seemed to be making her look older and haggard. Her hair didn't have the same glossy sheen that it usually had. Her normally pretty and sassy older sister looked tired and plain.

"Kelly, are you getting enough rest? You don't look so good," Harper said.

Her sister bristled. "What are you trying to say? I feel fine!"

But at her words, Yuna put down her utensils to look Kelly over.

"She's right, your color is looking off. I think you might be working too hard, honey."

"I don't know what you guys are talking about, I feel fine . . ."

"You look old, Kelly," Michael chimed in around a mouthful of chicken kebab.

Her fork clattering onto the table, Kelly jumped to her feet and ran over to look at the foyer mirror. With a big sigh of relief, she sat down again.

"That's just what makeup does, Michael," Kelly said. "It's supposed to make you look older."

Michael shook his head. "Not older, Kelly. Old. I don't like it."

Kelly laughed. "You're just a little kid. You don't know what you're talking about." Then she pushed back her chair, announced that she wasn't hungry, and excused herself from the table.

Harper's father, Peter, and cousin Leo seemed

confused by what had just happened, too.

"Um, guys, I don't think you should give Kelly such a hard time about her makeup," Peter said. "She really likes her job, and it's good for her."

"No, it's not, Dad," Harper responded vehemently. "She's wearing too much makeup, and she's spending too much time at that shop. It's not a good place for her."

"Now, Harper . . ."

"Peter, I think Harper is right," Yuna said quietly. Her eyebrows were furrowed in concern. "I really haven't liked her obsession with makeup. It's a bit much. And this is her junior year. I don't think she should spend so much time on a part-time job. She needs to focus on her academics."

"Yeah, Mom, you should tell her to quit."

"That's going too far," Peter replied. "No reason to force her to quit just yet. She wanted to make some money for the holidays."

Yuna was quiet and then let out a sigh. "We'll see."

Harper chewed on her lip. She knew this was a bad decision. But should she tell her parents what she'd seen?

After dinner, Harper called her grandmother and came clean about what she'd done. She felt really bad when her grandmother said, "Harper, you promised me you wouldn't do that!"

"I promised not to do it alone," Harper corrected. "I thought as long as Dayo was with me I'd be safe."

"Oh, Harper, you both could have been in terrible danger," her grandmother said in horror. "You must promise to never ever go there again!"

"I promise. But I don't know if that's enough . . . ," she replied.

"What do you mean?"

"At Kelly's makeup shop, I saw the thing again in a mirror," Harper admitted. "And I think it saw me, too."

"That is not good," her grandmother said, worry tingeing her voice.

"I'm sorry, Grandma."

"Harper, remember what Mrs. Devereux taught you! You must practice protecting yourself! You must not let your defenses down."

Alarmed, Harper agreed. "Does that mean I'm in danger?"

"Yes, you are in terrible danger! You've attracted a demon, and we must do everything in our power to protect you."

Deep in her heart, Harper had known it might be a demon, but she had tried to downplay it. Now she had to own the fact that this was all her fault.

"What can I do?"

"Do you still have the extra charm pouch I made for you this summer?"

Harper quickly opened her desk drawer and pulled out a pouch filled with salt, fennel, and sage. It was identical to the one hanging on her doorknob. Her grandmother had made her several extra pouches to keep handy.

"I have them, Grandma."

"Good. Put one under your pillow when you are sleeping."

Harper grabbed two of them and slid them under her pillow. Only then did she feel safe. Or at least a little safer.

"But that's not enough, you must work with Mrs. Devereux to strengthen your mind, Harper. Build a wall around your mind that will stay up at all times, even when you're sleeping."

"How can I do that?"

"Mrs. Devereux will teach you. I will send her to you right now."

As soon as she hung up the phone, Harper heard a voice.

Harper, I need to talk with you. Invite me in.

Shocked to hear Mrs. Devereux's voice in her

head, Harper opened her channel to let the spirit adviser in.

Mrs. Devereux appeared immediately, looking imposing in a black ball gown, with her hair pulled tight into a severe bun.

"Ma'am, how come you can pop in and out of Grandma's presence, but I have to invite you to see me?"

"Your grandmama and I have a spiritual connection that allows her channel to always be open to me. You do not. However, I could come to see you outside of this house whenever I want. But your grandma put a lot of protections on your home after Michael's possession so no spirit can enter without your direct permission. Not even me. And be glad of it."

"That's such a relief!" Harper could feel the weight of her fear lift off her shoulders. "I've been so worried!"

"You should be! You deliberately went against my direct orders and Madam's and put yourself in a dangerous situation!"

"But at least it can't get me here, right?"

The spiritual adviser sat down in midair and folded her hands across her abdomen.

"Harper, your powers have grown. You can enter the astral plane now. But you have not yet conquered your abilities to protect your mind. That means that while you are sleeping your mind is open and can project itself, leaving your spirit and your body completely vulnerable."

"I don't understand. What do you mean by that?"

"Your soul can leave your body and enter the astral plane while you are sleeping."

A chill went through Harper's body at Mrs. Devereux's words. Sometimes when she was dreaming, she would feel like she was floating away from her body. Was that what Mrs. Devereux was talking about?

"Exactly," Mrs. Devereux responded, reading her thoughts.

"Ugh, I may never sleep again."

"Unfortunately, that would be very bad also," Mrs. Devereux responded. "Humans need sleep, or they die."

"Gah!" Jumping to her feet, Harper crawled into her bed and pulled the covers over her head.

"You cannot hide from your fears, dearest," Mrs. Devereux said, in the most compassionate tone Harper had ever heard the ghost use. Harper lowered her blanket and sat up.

"I know I screwed up, ma'am," she said meekly. "I thought as long as Dayo was with me, I'd be safe. I don't think I really understood what the astral plane was. It's like another world, but it is just vast emptiness. And I felt so lost."

Mrs. Devereux listened intently as Harper described her entire experience and the demonic presence she'd met.

"Harper, a demon was lurking in the astral plane and caught sight of you. So, you then saw it again, in that mirror in the store?"

Harper nodded.

"Nothing happens randomly. The astral plane is so vast that nobody knows just how large it is. It may actually be infinite. So how is it that a demon would be lurking so close to where you were? How did it find you so quickly?"

"I did shout Dayo's name out loud," Harper said. She gasped in alarm. "Does that mean Dayo's in danger, too, because I said her name?"

"No, a name alone is not enough. But you, on the other hand . . ." Mrs. Devereux tightened her lips. "You said it appeared quickly, which means it was already nearby. But why? I'm worried that there is something we don't know."

"Well, now I'm really worried!"

Mrs. Devereux seemed lost in thought for a long

moment before focusing on Harper again.

"Listen, dearest, a demon in the astral plane is there for only two reasons. It is being kept in the astral plane against its will, or it thinks it has found a way to enter the human realm and is waiting for its chance."

"What do you mean, against its will?" Harper asked.

"There are humans who make deals with demons. Some are able to trick a demon, and then they bind them to do their bidding."

"How do humans have that kind of power?"

"Some are witches; others dabble in occult magic. But they will all end up regretting their actions," Mrs. Devereux stated. "There is always a terrible price to doing business with a demon."

Harper wondered who in Jeune had made a pact with a demon.

"We don't have time to concern ourselves with that right now," Mrs. Devereux admonished. "We must focus all our attention on making your defenses impenetrable. We must practice."

Taking a deep breath, Harper prepared herself to work on building a wall around her mind.

"Last time I told you to build a wall. But today,

what I want you to do is imagine a great, indestructible fortress wall wrapping completely around your thoughts. It will protect your mind so that nothing can enter it."

Harper shook her head. "I'm not sure what to do . . ."

Mrs. Devereux tapped a finger on her cheek. "I hate to make you remember this, but when you were first possessed by that ghost who started the fire, do you remember what she did and how it felt?"

It was a painful memory, one Harper could never forget. At her old school in New York, the ghost of a girl who had died in a fire fifty years earlier had haunted her. "Yes, it felt like she pushed into my head and took over. I felt like I was trapped in my own body."

"That must never happen again. Remember, this is about your thoughts, your mind, not your physical body. So go into your mind. Put yourself in a safe place and build a strong protective building around you so that nothing can enter your mind."

Nodding, Harper closed her eyes and imagined herself sitting on a flat grassy field with the sun shining bright above her. She then created thick metal walls around her in a large vast perimeter. It lifted high into the sky and formed a complete roof above her, capturing part of the sky and sunlight within its thick walls. This was her refuge. Leaning back on her hands, Harper wondered if this was enough.

"Excellent work, child! Now, the key is to keep it in place at all times."

They worked late into the night, and when Mrs. Devereux finally told Harper to stop, Harper almost didn't want to. She didn't want to fall asleep. She was too scared.

"I will stay with you, dear child," Mrs. Devereux said kindly. "I will watch over you tonight."

Relieved, Harper let herself succumb to the exhaustion that overwhelmed her.

THE POISONED MAKEUP

Sunday morning

Harper woke to the smell of bacon, eggs, and home fries. Her dad made the best breakfasts but only on the weekends. She looked around to see that she was once again alone. Mrs. Devereux had said she would leave at dawn. Feeling rested, Harper brushed her teeth and washed her face and ran downstairs to eat breakfast.

"Good morning!" Yuna smiled as Harper came downstairs.

Michael waved happily from his chair, already dipping his toast into his runny egg, and her dad, Peter, was in the kitchen cooking. "Do me a favor, Harper, and wake your sister up for breakfast."

Running back upstairs, Harper knocked on Kelly's door and then went in.

"Hey, Kelly, wake up! It's breakfast time!"

The lump in the bed didn't budge.

Harper went in and poked at the lump. "Come on, wake up! You know how Dad gets when we're late to his brunches."

Their dad was notorious for sulking if they didn't sit down immediately once he was done cooking.

Kelly moaned. It was such a pitiful sound that Harper looked closely at Kelly's naked face. Without makeup, Harper could see her sister's skin was splotchy and unhealthy. There was almost a yellowish tinge to it, as if she had jaundice or some other weird disease. Her usually pinkish red lips were pale, almost mauve. But not a pretty mauve. Like a worn-out, faded color.

"Hey, Kelly, you don't look good. Are you sick?"

Kelly opened her eyes, and Harper was shocked to see that the whites of her eyes looked slightly yellow. The dark brown irises were rimmed with gray.

"I'm okay," Kelly muttered. "Need to go to work."

"I don't think so!" Harper pushed her sister back into bed. Then she stepped out of the room to call down to her mom. "Mom, Kelly is sick!"

Immediately, Yuna came rushing upstairs to

check on her older daughter.

"Mom, I'm fine, just tired," Kelly mumbled. "I've got to go to work today."

"No, you are going to call in sick," Yuna replied firmly. "You have a fever, and you need to rest."

"But, Mom!"

"No buts, Kelly. You're staying home."

"What if they fire me?"

"Well, since that would make me happy, I don't see a problem."

Hanging by the door, Harper couldn't get over just how bad Kelly looked. It had first started when she began working at Jeune, and now it had gotten really bad. There was definitely something wrong with that makeup. Harper was sure of it.

After giving Kelly some medicine, Harper and her mom went down to the dining room to eat breakfast. Peter was sitting at the table, tapping his fingers restlessly.

"Your food is getting cold!"

"Sorry, Dad," Harper said as she started to dig into her food, which was actually still nice and hot.

"How's Kelly?" he asked Yuna.

"She must have caught a cold or something," Yuna said. "She has a slight fever, and she looks really pale."

"Mom, I went to the makeup shop with Dayo, and it gave me the absolute creeps," Harper said. "I don't think it's a good place for her to work."

"What do you mean, creeps?" Yuna asked. She was looking at Harper with alarm in her eyes.

"I sense that there's something bad in that house," Harper said. "I could feel it."

"Was it a ghost, Harper?" Michael asked.

Harper bit her lip. She didn't want to scare anyone, but she also didn't want her sister going back to that shop. "I think it might be something worse."

"Something worse?" Leo choked on his bacon. "Like from the island?"

"I don't know, and I don't want to find out, either," she replied. "All I know is that it scared me to death."

Harper saw her parents exchange worried glances.

"Well, I think it is a good idea for her to quit and focus on her studies, don't you agree, honey?" Yuna asked.

Peter was already nodding. "Clearly it is affecting her schoolwork if it's making her sick."

Harper breathed a sigh of relief. The one big change that had happened after their trip to Razu Island was that her parents finally believed her, and in her powers. They'd seen the bridge of souls that had lit up the sky after the demon monsters had been destroyed. When they came home, they'd gone to visit Grandma, and they had listened carefully to everything Harper explained about spirits. The hardest thing for them to accept was hearing that Michael could see ghosts also. They thought he was too young to deal with such frightening and traumatic events. But otherwise, they'd finally accepted that ghosts and demons existed.

After brunch, Leo and Michael followed Harper up to her room to ask her questions.

"Where did you see the scary thing?" Michael asked, sitting on the floor next to Harper. "Is it dangerous? Will it hurt Kelly?"

"As long as Kelly doesn't go back to work there, she should be safe."

"But what about other people? Aren't they in danger, too?"

This made Harper pause. Michael's little face was furrowed with concern, and even Leo was looking worried.

"I don't know," she admitted. "I've really only been worried about Kelly."

"That's not right, Harper!" Michael was alarmed. "We must help the peoples!"

"Hold up, Michael," Leo cut in. "We don't even

know what it is or if Harper can do anything about it. We need more information."

For once, Harper appreciated Leo's presence. Reluctantly, she told them about what happened, the demon on the astral plane and seeing it again in Jeune. She wasn't surprised when Leo exploded at her.

"First of all, Harper, you shouldn't have done that! You know how bad it was for me when I was haunted on the island! Why would you do it to another person?"

Michael folded his arms across his chest and glared at Leo. "Hey, don't yell at my sister! She did it to help you!"

"Well, I didn't need her help!"

Michael climbed into Harper's lap and gave her a hug. "It's okay, Harper. I knowed why you did it. You're a good person. But whatcha gonna do about the monster?"

"Yeah, Harper, what makes you sure it saw you?" Leo asked as he began to calm down again.

Harper shuddered. "Those red eyes. They looked straight at me like the demon knew me."

"And you said that the woman sitting in front of the mirror looked like her skin was aging. Do you think it had anything to do with the demon?"

She really had been trying not to think too much about the demon. But now she was realizing that there had to be some connection between the demon and these weird products that were making women look old and colorless.

"Mrs. Devereux said that a demon is only in the astral plane if it has been bound to a human or if it has found a way to enter the human realm," Harper thought out loud. "If I saw the demon in the mirror of the Jeune owner, then she must be the one who bound it."

"What does that mean?" Michael asked.

"Bound? Like she captured it and is making it work for her?" Leo asked.

"They are very powerful creatures, so if someone could bind one, they could make the demon do whatever they wanted."

Harper pulled up the memory of the owner, Jenna Graham, at the event. Black hair, paper-white skin, cold dead-fish eyes that were unnaturally green.

"Yeah, now that I think about it, that owner definitely looked like someone who could bind a demon," Harper said.

"But why? What would the demon do for her?" Leo asked.

"It must be some kind of magic," Harper said. "Everyone there thought the makeup looked beautiful and wonderful. But to me, it looked like it was aging them, stripping them of their natural color. There's some connection between that and the demon."

"We should test it out," Leo said. "Do you have any of the makeup?"

Harper shook her head. "Let me go grab some from Kelly's room."

"Don't let Kelly catch you," Michael warned. "She'll be angry!"

"Don't worry. Mom gave her some cold medicine. I'm pretty sure she's knocked out."

While Leo and Michael waited in the hallway, Harper snuck into Kelly's room and tiptoed over to the vanity that was next to her desk. There were makeup and skin products covering the entire surface. She looked for the black-and-purple Jeune bottles and quickly grabbed a few items and snuck back out.

Harper laid the bottles and containers on the floor and opened something called a cushion compact foundation.

"This was what they were using during the makeover," she said. "It made their skin age like leather and dulled their complexion." She thought back to that day. The young women had been pretty and bright, but after the makeovers, they'd resembled wax statues.

Leo picked it up and examined it closely. "Maybe you should try it on, Harper."

"No way, Harper, don't do it. That's bad stuff!" Michael was waving his hands furiously. "I don't want Harper to get sick, too."

Harper reached over and gave Michael a big hug. "Don't worry, buddy, I won't get sick," she reassured him. "I'm not gonna put it on my face. I just want to test it on my hand and check it out. I'm thinking you and I might be able to see something if it's related to spirit stuff."

Michael clung to Harper's arm. "But are you sure it won't hurt you?"

She patted his back and reached for her bag of bells. Opening it up, she pulled out a spray bottle of holy water. It came in handy for warding off aggressive spirits.

"If there's anything spirit-related, this should help."

Michael nodded and sat back.

Taking the compact out of its box, Harper flipped it open and used the cushion to depress some liquid foundation onto the pad.

"Ew, what is that stuff?" Leo asked.

"It's foundation," Harper replied. "It says it's for evening out your complexion."

"What does that mean?"

Harper shrugged. "Beats me."

Carefully looking at the liquid that had now soaked into the cushion, Harper thought she saw slight fumes rise.

"Michael, do you see something like smoke?"

Her little brother stood up and stuck his face as close to the compact as possible. He shook his head sadly.

"I didn't see nothing, Harper."

"Maybe I was wrong," Harper replied. "Okay, here goes."

She pulled the floor lamp closer to brighten the area where they were sitting. Taking the pad, she wiped the foundation on the back of her hand. And then all three of them stared intently at it.

"Does it hurt?" Michael asked.

"No, but it kind of tingles."

"Tingle? Is makeup supposed to tingle?" Leo asked in alarm.

"I don't know," Harper said. "But I don't think so."

Suddenly, Michael gasped. "Look, Harper, smoke!"

In the brightness of the light, faint fumes rose from the spot where the pinkish-beige-colored makeup covered Harper's hand. For a split second, Harper could see her skin under the foundation wrinkling like a prune. But then a strange, dreamy sensation overwhelmed Harper.

Don't you want to look beautiful?

You need more Jeune.

Don't you want to feel young again?

Jeune will make you feel young and pretty.

The voice was sweet and charming and so compelling. *Of course, Jeune will make me look beautiful*, Harper thought. As if she was in a trance, Harper picked up the compact and looked into its tiny mirror.

"I want to look beautiful," she whispered as she raised the cushion to her face.

"What are you doing?" Leo grabbed her hand to stop her.

"I just need to put some on my face," Harper said, in a vague manner. "I need it. I need more."

Leo snatched the cushion and compact out of her hand.

"We have to get this makeup off," Leo said.

Michael grabbed the spray bottle of holy water and immediately drenched Harper's hand just as Leo rubbed it all off with a bunch of tissues.

The peculiar trance Harper was in abruptly dissipated.

"Wow, that was weird," Harper whispered. She looked at her hand. The tingling had stopped, and the skin looked back to normal.

"What happened?" Leo asked. "You were acting strange."

Michael nodded and hugged her. "You scared me, Harper."

"I'm sorry," Harper said. "I heard this voice in my head—it was so charming, so inviting, and it was persuading me to put more makeup on."

"That's bizarre," Leo remarked.

Staring down at the compact, now on the floor, Harper could almost hear that seductive voice again.

"At first, there were these fumes and then I saw my skin wrinkle, but the voice started talking right away."

"But I didn't see any smoke." Leo shook his head.

"I did! I sawd it!" Michael said. "It looked like poison!"

"Michael, you don't even know what poison looks like." Harper smiled slightly.

Her little brother stuck out his lower lip. "It's

poison," he insisted. "It made you act strange."

"Well, it's definitely bad, whatever it is," Harper replied.

"But what is it, and why is this makeup company using it?" Leo asked.

"And what's going to happen to Kelly?" Michael asked. "She's been using the bad makeup every day for years!"

"Probably more like a month," Harper said.

"That's too long!" Michael cried out. "We have to help her!"

Patting him on the back, Harper nodded. "Of course, Michael. She's our sister."

But how, was the big question. And would it mean that Harper would have to go back into the astral plane? Just the thought of it chilled her to the bone. "I need to go talk to Grandma and Mrs. D, right away."

A WITCH

That afternoon, Harper asked her grandmother to video chat with her while she was with Mrs. Devereux. She set up her laptop and dialed her grandma.

"Hello, Harper! I'm using your auntie's laptop. Can you see me?"

"Yep! Hi, Grandma! Mrs. Devereux is here also."

"Good evening, madam," Mrs. Devereux said.

"Good evening, Dominique."

Harper did a double take. "You can see her on the video screen?"

"No, but I can hear her communicating with

me," her grandmother replied.

"We have our own channel, Harper," Mrs. Devereux said.

"So why did you need to see us together?" Grandma Lee asked.

"It's about Kelly and that demon," Harper said. Pulling out the Jeune makeup she took from Kelly's room, Harper opened it to show them. "I'm pretty sure there is demon magic inside the makeup."

"How do you know?" her grandmother asked.

Harper explained about her experiment with the makeup, how she fell into a trance and heard that persuasive voice that had taken hold of her.

Grandma gasped, and Mrs. Devereux cursed in her native Creole French. Or at least Harper thought it sounded like cursing.

Mrs. Devereux carefully looked at the makeup and frowned.

"I know what this is," she said. "This is not demon-based. This is the darkest magic, and it must be from a very powerful witch."

Harper's mouth dropped open. "A real witch?"

Mrs. Devereux gave Harper quite a look, reminding her who she was in her prior life.

"And of course you would know," Harper said meekly. Mrs. Devereux had been an extremely powerful witch and psychic when she was alive.

"I recognize this magic," Mrs. Devereux continued. "It's a youth-stealing spell."

In shock, Harper sucked her breath in between her teeth, causing a sharp whistling sound.

"But what about my sister, Kelly? Is that why she looks so terrible? What's going to happen to her?"

"This is a considerably weakened spell. It's only meant to steal a little youth at a time. A day, at most, with each application," Mrs. Devereux said. "If she's been wearing it every day for a month, it would have stolen exactly that much youth from her."

That made sense to Harper. If the makeup stole so much youth that it visibly aged a person, then people would stop buying it. But just a little bit wouldn't be noticed.

"But then why does she look so bad?" Harper asked. She looked at the other makeup she had taken from Kelly's room. Opening a lipstick and an eye shadow, she showed them to Mrs. D. "Do these have the magic spell also?"

The spiritual adviser nodded.

"Then if she is using several products at a time, and they are all stealing a day of youth from her, she's lost far more than a month," Mrs. Devereux said.

Harper remembered the makeover event at the

store. There were at least a hundred people buying makeup that day.

Harper slapped her hand over her mouth to bite back her angry words. "The Jeune store here is their first one. I remember Kelly saying that if it does well, they would expand nationwide. Maybe even globally."

"Goodness gracious!" Grandma Lee looked horrified. "But that means they will be siphoning life from possibly millions of people!

"What do we do?" Grandma Lee was beside herself. "We must stop this!"

"I'll go to the store and see what I can discover," Mrs. Devereux said. "We need to know what exactly we are dealing with."

"Do be careful, Dominique," Grandma Lee said.

"Always," Mrs. Devereux replied. And then she vanished.

A few hours later, Harper got a call from her grandmother.

"Grandma, did Mrs. Devereux come back?"

"Yes, she's with me now," her grandma replied. "She was unable to snoop around too much because that demon acts as an alarm. She was in the basement for only a few minutes when the demon appeared in the mirrors and called out to its master."

"Master? You mean the witch?"

"I believe so," her grandmother replied.

"So did she see her?"

"Yes, she was a white woman with very dark hair and unnatural green eyes."

"That's Jenna Graham," Harper said. "I knew it had to be her! Did Mrs. Devereux see anything important?"

"No, she didn't have time."

"So, what do we do?"

"There's no choice but for Kelly to go back to work. She needs to bring something of Jenna's home so you can read it, Harper."

"But Mom told Kelly she couldn't go back to work!"

Grandma Lee sighed. "Well then, I don't know what we are going to do."

"Maybe I can find an excuse for her to go back."

Just then, there was a loud knocking on Harper's door and it swung open. Harper hurriedly got off the call as Kelly marched in, looking furious.

"Harper, did you take my makeup?"

Before Harper could answer, Kelly spotted the pile of her makeup on Harper's floor.

"What the heck?" Kelly picked up her compact and waved it in Harper's face. "Do you know how expensive this is? I don't want you touching my stuff!"

Kelly swept up her things with angry, herky-jerky motions, then stormed out.

"Hey, Kelly, you shouldn't wear that stuff. It's not good for you!" Harper said as she followed Kelly back to her room.

"Shut up, Harper! And stay out of my room!"

With that, Kelly slammed the door in Harper's face.

Someone was tugging on Harper's sleeve. She glanced down to see Michael at her side.

"Did Kelly yell at you about the makeup?"

"Yeah," Harper sighed.

"It's okay, Harper," Michael said as he led her to his room. "I heared her yell at Mommy and Daddy, too. She said she was going to work and no one could stop her."

"Oh, wow! What did Mom and Dad say?" Harper asked.

Michael pulled Harper down to sit on the floor with him and started pouring his Lego pieces in front of her.

"Nothing. They both looked like this." Michael made a shocked face, with his mouth hanging open. "And then Kelly went upstairs like an elephant." He banged his feet on the floor.

"Okay, I get it," Harper laughed. "Did they say anything after?"

"They told me to go upstairs and ask you to play with me."

"They did?" Harper asked in surprise.

Michael grinned. "No. But you will anyway, won't you?"

"Sure, buddy," Harper replied. "Anything for you."

As her brother chattered away about what he wanted to build with his Legos, Harper thought back to what her grandmother had said. They needed Kelly to go back to work and get something of Jenna's. But Kelly was definitely not in the mood to help Harper.

There was no choice. Harper would have to go back to Jeune and face the demon once again.

Harper shuddered.

BACK TO JEUNE
Monday

Dayo was bundled up tight in her brand-new pink puffy coat and waiting for Harper outside of her house as Harper pulled up on her bicycle.

"You look like a big cotton candy cone!" Harper laughed.

Dayo stuck her tongue out. "At least I'll be warm!"

"I like it! There's no way anyone can miss seeing you," Harper said.

"You're just jealous of my new coat!"

"I am. Mine's very boring next to yours." Harper shook her head sadly as she stared down at her heavy black winter coat and white scarf.

"That's why you've got me as your BFF! I'm the

fashionable one!" Dayo gave Harper a twinkling smile as they both began riding to school.

"Where's Leo?" Dayo asked.

"He said he wanted to go to school early."

"So is Kelly going to Jeune today?" Dayo asked.

Harper nodded. She'd called Dayo last night to fill her in on everything that had happened. "She didn't even eat breakfast this morning. She told my parents she was going straight to work after school and then walked out of the house. And my parents didn't try to stop her or anything. It was so weird."

"So what's the plan? Do we go there after school also?"

"I'm supposed to pick up Michael today," Harper said. "Apparently his tae kwon do class was canceled. I have to babysit him after school."

"What about Leo? Can't he watch him?"

"Hey, yeah! Let's ask him. But isn't it supposed to rain later?"

"We can take the bus," Dayo said. "It's a few blocks from my house, and there's a stop on the same block as Jeune."

"Really? How much is it?"

"It's free for us since we're students. Just bring your student ID."

"Awesome! Let's do it!"

"But, Harper, aren't you afraid of that demon in the mirror?"

"Of course I am," Harper replied. "But this is bigger than my fear. I don't have a choice."

"You're so brave, Harper," Dayo said admiringly. "I'm so glad we're friends."

"Not as glad as I am, Dayo," Harper said. "You're the best thing that happened to me."

The friends smiled in perfect harmony.

At their lunch table, Dayo and Harper sat next to Maya and Judy, who were the first ones in the cafeteria.

"Where is everybody?" Dayo asked.

Before anyone could answer, Tyler and Gabby appeared. Tyler collapsed dramatically next to Harper and yanked at her sleeve.

"You will not believe what I heard!"

Shaking her head, Gabby sat across from him and said, "Just tell us already!"

Tyler clapped his hands in delight, leaned forward, and motioned them into a huddle.

"Apparently, Joey Ramos is being haunted by an evil ghost and he's so scared to be alone that he's been sleeping with his parents like a baby!"

Everyone at the table burst into giggles.

"He thinks he's being haunted?"

"What a loser!"

"No way, this can't be true," Maya said. "I mean, who believes in ghosts?"

"Apparently Joey does," Devon said as he slid into the seat between Maya and Judy. Judy rolled her eyes but made room. "He told the whole soccer team about ghosts and wants all of us to carry crosses and bottles of holy water."

As the discussion turned to ghosts and whether or not they were real, Dayo and Harper looked at each other and tried hard not to laugh.

"Well, if anyone was going to be haunted by an evil ghost, I'm glad it was Joey Ramos," Tyler proclaimed.

After school, Harper and Dayo waited for Leo. This time, none of the bullies followed him outside.

"Hey, Leo, did that Joey guy bother you today?"

Leo grinned and shook his head. "Whatever you did spooked him good. He was real quiet and didn't bother me at all."

"Oh, so you owe her, then, right?" Dayo asked.

He shrugged and agreed.

"Great, can you watch Michael for a few hours today after we pick him up?" Harper quickly asked.

"Yeah, sure, but why?"

They quickly explained what was going on and

watched as Leo's eyebrows rose in alarm.

"Are you sure this is a good idea?"

"Grandma said it was the only way," Harper responded.

Leo was shaking his head. "I just don't have a good feeling about this."

"Don't worry," Dayo cut in. "I'll be there with her."

Harper beamed at Dayo. "Thank you, my best friend."

"You're welcome, my best friend!"

Rolling his eyes, Leo got on his bike and rode away.

"Don't forget, you're watching Michael!"

Leo waved his hand in acknowledgment.

At Michael's school, Harper left her bike with Dayo and went up to the door to pick up her brother. All the kindergartners waved good-bye as she walked Michael out of the school. When he saw Dayo, he jumped into her arms and gave her a big hug. Then he turned to Harper and let out a heavy sigh. "Harper, I'm tired today."

"Why's that, buddy?"

"Because I run-ded and run-ded a lot in gym. So I'm too tired to walk home."

"Uh-oh, what are we gonna do, then?" Harper asked.

"Well, Mommy said you couldn't ride with me in the basket. But what if you walked and I rided in the basket?"

"Oh, he's so smart," Dayo giggled.

"This is what happens when you have lawyers for parents." Harper shook her head. "Okay, buddy, but you have to hold on tight!"

"Yippee!"

Harper lifted Michael into her front basket as Dayo held the bike steady. He sat scrunched up sideways in the wire basket.

"I think you grew, Michael," Harper said. "You barely fit anymore."

"I'm a big boy!"

Laughing, the two friends walked their bikes as Michael chattered away about his day.

Dropping Michael off with Leo, Harper and Dayo went to Dayo's house to leave her bike and walk over to the bus stop. Fortified by Mrs. Clayton's delicious cookies, the girls were ready for their mission.

Twenty minutes later, they were walking across the street toward Jeune, and Harper's unease grew.

"You okay, Harper?" Dayo asked in concern.

"I'm fine," Harper answered. "Just a little nervous."

Dayo squeezed Harper's hand, and the girls linked arms as they approached the store.

Inside the shop, it was busy with holiday shoppers. Big signs were plastered all over the walls and shelves listing special sales.

"What are you doing here?"

Both Dayo and Harper jumped at hearing Kelly's hostile voice.

"Hey, Kelly. Harper came with me to buy a Christmas present for my mom," Dayo replied.

Visibly softening at Dayo's words, Kelly smiled warmly. "That's great! What were you thinking of? I'm sure I can help you."

"I'm not quite sure. I was going to look around a bit and then come and ask you for help, if that's okay?"

"Sure," Kelly said. "Just to let you know, purple signs are for ten percent off and the pink signs are for twenty-five percent off. Just let me know when you need me."

Once Kelly left them, Harper let out her breath in a big whoosh.

"Good thinking, Dayo! She surprised me."

Dayo patted Harper on the back. "It's all good. Now let's figure out how to get what we came for."

"We should have asked Kelly if Jenna was here," Harper said.

"No need," Dayo whispered. "Look."

At the back of the shop where the stage was, Jenna was talking to a few customers who were getting makeovers. She was clearly talking up her products, and they were eager to purchase them.

"What is it you need to get, Harper?"

"I need something of hers, or at the very least something that only she touches."

"That's gonna be hard," Dayo said. Jenna was touching a lot of things but also passing them on to customers. Harper heaved a frustrated breath.

"It's too busy because of the holiday sales."

Dayo nudged Harper. "Look!"

Kelly was talking to Jenna, and they were heading to the curtained back room.

"I'm going to follow them, and you distract her," Harper said as she pointed at the salesperson standing near the exit.

"Got it. Be careful, Harper."

The girls walked toward the door, with Dayo stopping to ask the salesperson a question and Harper slipping through the curtain. She found herself in a storage room that was filled with boxes of Jeune products. There must have been thousands in that room alone. Every single one would steal days from the person who used it. This had to be stopped. At the other end of the storage room was a door that led to the small landing of a staircase. She could hear Kelly's muffled voice coming from upstairs. Harper tiptoed up the stairs and stopped before the landing. She could see Kelly's back and part of Jenna's arm.

"I don't know what to do," Kelly was saying. "They keep insisting I have to quit, but I don't want to! I want to keep working with you!"

"Of course! I need you, Kelly. You're the future of this company," Jenna said. Her voice was soothing and almost hypnotic. "If I had a daughter, I would have wanted her to be just like you, Kelly."

"Really? I wish you were my mom also," Kelly said. "I wouldn't have to be constantly yelled at and told what to do. They're so unreasonable! And they don't care about me at all. They just want me to do what *they* think is right, but never think about what I need, what I want to do."

Harper had to bite back her anger at Kelly's words.

"Oh, my poor girl! If only there was something I could do for you," Jenna soothed.

"I just want to be here with you," Kelly responded.

"Yes, dear, always. In fact, I have something for you, to show you just how important you are to me," Jenna said.

Harper peered up to find out what Jenna was

giving Kelly, but she couldn't see.

"Isn't that your cameo?" Kelly said breathlessly.

"Yes, I've had it for years," Jenna replied. "But I want you to have it now."

"Oh, but I couldn't!"

"I insist!"

Peeking over the landing, Harper could see Jenna's hands placing something around Kelly's neck.

"It's yours now, a token of my love and gratitude for you."

"Thank you, Jenna, I'll treasure it always!"

Not wanting to push her luck, Harper snuck back down the stairs and hurried through the storage room and out the curtained door.

"Excuse me, what are you doing? That's for employees only," the salesperson said, her face clouded in disapproval. Her name tag read "Becky, beauty adviser."

"I'm so sorry, I was looking for the bathroom," Harper replied.

"We don't have any public bathrooms," Becky said.

"I'd better go, then. I have an emergency," Harper said. Catching Dayo's eye, she started toward the front door.

"Wait a minute. Can I see your bag?" Becky stepped in front of Harper.

"I don't have a bag," Harper replied. She opened her coat. "See."

The beauty adviser continued to look at Harper suspiciously. "Can you empty out your pockets?"

Dayo walked over. "What's going on, Harper?"

The woman turned her suspicious eye to Dayo. "Please empty your pockets also."

Harper was furious. "Listen, we didn't steal anything!"

"Maybe we should go to the back and have both your parents come in," Becky said sternly.

"What's going on?" Kelly asked.

"Kelly, she's accusing us of stealing!"

"Do you know these girls?" Becky asked in surprise.

"Yes, this is my sister, Harper, and her best friend, Dayo," Kelly replied. "I will vouch for them. They would never steal anything."

"Sisters? You don't look alike at all." Without apologizing, Becky walked away, ignoring Dayo's and Harper's angry glares.

"What happened?"

"We were heading toward the door, and she stopped us," Harper replied. "And it felt really bad and really racist."

Frowning, Kelly turned to look at the other woman. "I always got a bit of a bad vibe from her," she remarked.

"That's cause she's racist," Harper retorted.

"Yep," Dayo agreed. "I actually saw some white girls stealing lipsticks, but she didn't say a word to them when they left. But she stops the one Black girl and the one Asian girl in the store. That's just messed up."

"I'm really sorry about that, guys. I'll talk to her about it."

Not wanting Becky to tell Kelly that she'd seen Harper come out of the storage room, Harper waved her hands.

"That's okay, Kelly. Don't say anything. It'll make work uncomfortable for you."

Kelly looked troubled. "But still, I should report it."

At that moment, Harper noticed the cameo necklace Kelly was wearing.

"Whoa, where'd you get that necklace? It's beautiful."

Kelly smiled. "My boss gave it to me."

Harper and Dayo crowded closer to take a better look.

"She must really like you a lot!" Dayo said. "It looks pretty expensive."

A weird, daydreamy look set on Kelly's face. "It was hers, but she gave it to me to remind me of how much she depends on me."

Harper exchanged a knowing glance with Dayo.

"That's awesome, Kelly! Well, you'd better get back to work, and we're gonna head home now."

"Okay, see you later," Kelly replied, the weird expression still on her face.

Harper and Dayo quickly left the shop and walked to the bus stop.

"That doesn't make any sense," Harper said. "Why would Jenna give Kelly an expensive piece of jewelry?"

"Wasn't she wearing it when we saw her at the makeover event?" Dayo asked.

"You're right. She was," Harper exclaimed. "I just need to sneak into Kelly's room and touch it while she's sleeping."

"Be careful," Dayo said.

Harper nodded. "Don't worry. I've got this. I'll be fine."

THE CURSED CAMEO

Harper's alarm rang at three a.m. Bleary-eyed, she shut off her alarm and wondered why in the world she'd set it so early. It took several minutes of blinking for her to finally remember Kelly and the cameo necklace.

She crept down the hallway toward Kelly's room and carefully opened the door. Soft snores were emanating from the bed. Letting out the breath she was holding, Harper snuck over to her sister's bureau and found the cameo carefully placed on the dresser top.

Picking it up, Harper grasped the cameo tightly in her hands and closed her eyes.

Images came vividly alive and flashed through Harper's mind at lightning speed. So many that she couldn't make out any of it. It was too much. But the pain and the emotions came through with a force. Rage and pain. So much pain. So many memories! How could one person have this many? Was the cameo owned by others also? The visions were too fast. She was getting dizzy.

Someone was sobbing. Harper latched onto the sound to trace it to a memory.

A young woman is crying. Harper can see she is dressed in really old-fashioned clothing with a white lace cap, like the Puritans wore. An older dark-haired woman with green eyes, like Jenna, comforts the girl. Harper notices that she is wearing the same cameo Jenna gave Kelly. But instead of a chain, it is tied on by a black ribbon.

"I'm sorry, Mistress Wentworth! 'Twas an accident! I did not mean to reveal your secret to Deacon Jamison!"

"There, there, Rebecca, do not fear."

"But the deacon! He is coming! I came to warn thee! Thou must leave now, mistress!"

"There's naught to worry about, dearest

Rebecca." The older woman took off her cameo and tied it on Rebecca's neck.

"Thy treasured possession. Mistress, why art thou giving it to me?"

"Because thou wilt take good care of it from here on," Mistress replied. Her green eyes darkened, and she began to whisper in a language Harper didn't understand. Rebecca swayed in the older woman's arms and convulsed as if she was having a seizure. Then Rebecca's mouth opened. The mistress quickly breathed in the bright white essence coming from Rebecca and expelled a green essence into Rebecca's mouth. Suddenly, the older woman collapsed in Rebecca's arms.

Rebecca lay the woman on the bed and caressed her face. With a secretive smile, she said something strange.

As she looked down on the older woman, she whispered, "I must thank thee for thy service, fair Rebecca."

The older woman opened her eyes, but they were no longer green; they were a pale blue, filled with panic. She was trying to move but seemed paralyzed. Agonizing guttural sounds were coming from her throat, and her eyes were wild.

"Do not fight so hard, dearest, thou art frozen by my spell. It is my most powerful magic! A spell that switches the souls. I had not planned on using this until I was much older. Once used, it must be repeated at the same age. But forty is old enough. And 'tis fitting that thou art the first, as thou hast brought the witch hunters to my door."

Rebecca turned, and Harper saw that her eyes had changed to the same green eyes as Jenna. This new person in Rebecca's form picked up a large black bag.

"Fare thee well, Rebecca," the woman said. Wrapping a black cloak around her shoulders, she quickly departed, hiding in the woods near the house and waiting. Not very much later, a group of men with torches and weapons appeared in front of the house shouting for the witch.

"Constance Wentworth! Show yourself, witch!"

Several kicked down the door and went inside while the others threw a rope with a noose around a large branch of the tree in front of the house.

They dragged the witch out of the house and placed the noose around her head. They asked her if she had any last words, but the soul of the girl Rebecca, trapped in the witch's body, still could not speak or move.

*Heaving her high up onto the branch, they hung
her until her feet stopped quivering. Only then did
the real witch silently fade into the darkness and
disappear.*

Gasping for air, Harper released the cameo, and
it fell on the carpet. But Harper was so unnerved
by what she saw, she couldn't bear to touch it again.
Leaving it on the floor, she quickly sped out of Kelly's
room.

Safe in her bed, Harper put a hand over her
rapidly beating heart. What did this all mean? Did
Jenna give Kelly the cameo so that she could take
over her body? Was that how she was able to live for
so long? Taking over the bodies of young teenage
girls? Harper shuddered. What did she mean that
the spell had to be repeated at the same age? Forty?
She looked forty now! That meant she would need to
switch bodies soon. Kelly was in terrible danger!

"The cameo!" Harper thought it had to be of
importance. Maybe Jenna needed it to help with the
soul switch.

Jumping out of bed, Harper hurried back to Kelly's
room to steal the cameo. As she picked it up from the
floor where she'd dropped it, Kelly suddenly woke up.

"What are you doing?"

Kelly was out of bed and in front of Harper in a flash. Kelly saw the cameo in Harper's hand and snatched it away.

"Harper, stop stealing my things!"

"But, Kelly, this is dangerous! You can't wear it!"

"Get out of my room!"

"No, Kelly! You have to believe me! You can't wear it! It's dangerous!"

Harper reached out to take the cameo back when Kelly hit her hard across the face and shoved her out of her room.

"Don't ever come into my room again!"

Kelly slammed the door. Stunned by the violence, Harper just stood gaping, her hand covering her stinging eye.

Yuna came out of her bedroom to check on the commotion.

"Honey, are you okay? What happened?"

So many thoughts were raging through Harper's brain, but the first thought she had was that there was no way her mother would believe her.

Turning to hide her face, Harper said, "It's okay, Mom. I'm going to bed."

She quickly shuffled down the hallway before her mom could ask any more questions. In her room, Harper looked at her face. It was red and already swollen. The corner of her eye hurt like it was going to bruise. She couldn't believe how hard Kelly had struck her. Actually, she couldn't believe that her sister had hit her at all! Tired and bruised both physically and emotionally, Harper slid into bed and wrapped herself tight in her comforter. She'd worry tomorrow about how she would save her sister.

THE WITCH, THE DEMON, AND THE ASTRAL PLANE

Tuesday morning

*H*arper found herself floating in a dark room. She wasn't sure if she was dreaming or if she'd traveled the astral plane again. But if she'd left her body, where was she? Trying not to panic, Harper took a careful look at her surroundings. She was in some kind of storage room. A bright flashing light caught her attention. Cautiously, she moved forward but stopped as soon as she realized someone was there.

Beyond the storage area, Harper could see the figure of a woman kneeling in front of a large glass chamber filled with bright flashing lights. The chamber was separated into two compartments. In the top compartment, hundreds of small lights would appear and coalesce into a large colorful bead. The bottom compartment of the chamber was where all the beads were collected. The woman was gathering all the large beads and placing them into several velvet-lined boxes. When she was done, the bottom chamber was empty, until another bead dropped from the top.

"Such a terrible amount of effort just to get a few years into a pretty bead. This new venture of yours is tedious and drains my powers."

The woman turned to face a large mirror, where the red eyes of a demon gleamed.

"Quit complaining, Andras. It's my magic in these products that absorbs youth," Jenna remarked. "All you do is gather it here."

"Darling, do you have any idea how much power it takes to direct all your spells into this compartment?" Andras asked. "There must be literally tens of thousands of products being used every day! And I'm the one channeling them all and creating your little youth beads. You've spread my magic out so much it weakens me terribly. And for what? I'll never understand your insatiable need for money when you already have magic."

"It's not about money, Andras," Jenna retorted.

"I get enough of that already. Jeune is about providing favors to the most powerful people in the world."

"Favors? Your youth beads are favors? I thought you sold them to the highest bidder," the demon Andras drawled.

"I give them to people who will help me transform to my next body," Jenna said. "You're a demon. You couldn't understand the nature of all the ridiculous legal and business dealings that humans must deal with. It was much easier in the past, when all you needed was gold to prove who you were."

"Ah, if only your spell didn't need you to change bodies at forty. Another ten years could have made such a difference."

"Don't remind me! For nearly four hundred years, switching bodies and starting all over again every twenty years has been incredibly troublesome! Curse that wretched Rebecca girl! She started it all!" Jenna complained. "But this time my new body will solve that problem."

"Yes, the Raine child will be decidedly more useful," the demon laughed.

"However, she will come with a host of new legal problems I've not had to deal with before. This is why I need all the favors I can collect." Jenna waved *a red bead in front of the demon in the mirror.*

"But your fortieth year is ending fast. You best hurry."

"For this particular spell to be most effective, it must be cast the night of a full moon."

"Well, that's terribly convenient for you," the demon drawled. "Everything is lining up quite nicely. And when you change bodies this last time, do not forget our deal."

The demon's voice turned menacing.

"Harper! You're late!"

Harper felt herself being rapidly pulled back into her body. She opened her eyes just as Michael climbed into her bed and jumped on her.

"Wake up, sleepyhead!"

She was horrified to realize that she'd left her body and had traveled to Jeune. Had it not been for Michael . . . Well, she didn't want to even think about it.

As she sat up, Michael gasped. "What happened to your face?"

Putting a hand to her face, Harper realized it was swollen and painful.

"Huh, I should have iced it," Harper murmured as she walked over to her mirror and did a double take. Her left eye was black-and-blue, and her cheek looked like she was storing nuts in it.

"Did a ghost do that to you?" Michael whispered, his little face overcome with worry.

"No, this was . . . an accident."

"Well, you'd better come down right away and show Mommy," he said as he ran out of her door yelling at the top of his lungs.

"Mommy! Harper has a black eye, and her face is all puffy!"

Harper groaned. She was already not feeling up to going to school. But hearing him describe her face sent her flying back into bed. A few minutes passed, and then she heard her mom knock softly and enter.

"Michael said you're hurt," her mother said. "Honey, let me see."

Harper pulled down her covers.

"Oh my goodness! What happened?" Yuna was shocked.

"It was an accident," Harper muttered. "I fell out of bed."

She didn't want to tell her mother that Kelly did it. She still had to figure out how to save her.

Yuna placed an ice pack on Harper's injuries. "We need to take you to the doctor right now!"

Alarmed, Harper sat up and waved her hands.

"No, Mom! I'm fine, really! It just aches a little, but it doesn't even hurt that much!" Harper hated going to doctors and hospitals more than anything else in the world. She had too many bad memories from those long-ago days when she was possessed by evil ghosts.

Her mother sat down on the bed.

"Are you sure? Maybe we have to check and make sure you don't have a concussion?"

Harper shook her head. "Mom, I didn't hit my head, I hit my cheek. It aches, but I'll survive. I just need to sleep some more."

"All right, then. I can work from home. Why don't you go back to sleep? I'll let your school know you're staying home today, and I'll ask Leo to pick up Michael."

"Thanks, Mom," Harper said. When her mother left, she heaved a shuddering breath of relief. Just the idea of going to the hospital had made her heart beat rapidly. She knew she had to get over her fear of them, but it would take a long time.

Harper closed her eyes and fell asleep.

She was floating in darkness. She had no clue where she was. Looking all around her, all she saw was a vast, dark nothingness. A terrible feeling overcame her. Was she back in the astral plane?

Had her soul floated out of her body and come on its own? Alarmed and extremely frightened, she tried to find the light back to her body. She searched and searched, spinning in circles, until she finally caught a pinprick of light. As she headed for it, what she had feared came true.

"Is that you? Little one? Are you the tasty morsel I missed last time?"

The voice of the demon came from up ahead, where the light was. Afraid to see those red eyes, Harper whirled away.

"Come back, little one!"

Frantic, Harper immediately thought of her grandmother, cozy in her room at her aunt's house. As soon as she visualized the memory, she popped out into her grandmother's room.

"Grandma!" Harper shouted, waking her grandmother up from her nap and sending Monty into a frenzy of barking.

"Harper! You're not supposed to use the astral plane!"

"I know—I wasn't! I was asleep, and then suddenly I was there. I was trying to get back, but it seemed so far, and the demon was coming for me. So I just thought of you, and here I am. I'm sorry."

"Oh, Harper, that's why we've been teaching you

to build the wall. What happened?"

"I was so tired, and I was in pain and worried about Kelly. And it was just a nap, so I didn't think I needed the wall."

Grandma Lee was shaking her head. "You always need it. You must train yourself to do it even when you are absolutely exhausted because that is when you most need it."

"I know, I know! I promise I will, Grandma!"

"You have to go back right away. You can't leave your body exposed and alone."

"But the demon is out there waiting for me!"

"All right, calm down, Harper. Take some deep breaths. It's no different than coming to see me. Visualize your room. Then see yourself sleeping in your bed. Focus."

Harper closed her eyes. She could see her room and her bed. She focused on her thick blue comforter with purple forget-me-nots dotted on it. She imagined herself wrapped in its warmth and softness and suddenly . . .

Harper opened her eyes, and she was back in her bed. Heaving a relieved sigh, she heard her phone ring and knew it was her grandma.

"Grandma, I'm back!"

"Harper, thank goodness!" Her grandmother's voice still sounded stressed. "Okay, now tell me everything that happened! Everything before you floated into the astral plane."

In a gush of words, Harper was finally able to unload the burden of everything that had happened since going to Jeune and the conversation she'd overheard between Jenna and the demon. When she was done, her grandmother was silent for a long while.

"Grandma? Did you listen to me?"

"Yes, dear, and we are very concerned. The full moon is this Friday night."

"Is Mrs. Devereux with you?" Harper asked.

"Yes, and she would like to come talk to you now."

Harper shook her head. "That's not a good idea. Mom's working from home today because I stayed home sick. She'll be checking up on me a lot."

"Okay, then. Tonight."

Harper agreed. "But what do we do about Kelly?"

"Let me talk with Mrs. Devereux, and I'll let you know."

Unhappy about the wait, Harper hung up the phone just as her mother knocked on her door.

"I've brought you a fresh ice pack and a little snack," Yuna said. "You didn't eat breakfast."

Happy for the distraction and too scared to sleep again, Harper sat up and enjoyed the chocolate croissant and milk her mother had brought her.

Yuna sat next to the bed and gently touched Harper's bruised cheek.

"Do you want to tell me what really happened?"

Avoiding her mother's eyes, Harper squirmed internally. She hated lying to her.

"It was all my fault," Harper said. "I fell and hit my face."

"I guess you must have hit the end table," Yuna remarked. "You're so lucky it wasn't any closer to your eye!"

It's a good thing Kelly didn't hit me any closer to my eye, Harper thought grudgingly. *If I told on her, she'd be grounded for a year.*

That knowledge gave her a little satisfaction, and she bit into her croissant with gusto.

"Eat over the tray or you'll get crumbs in your bed."

Harper picked at the crumbs on her pajama shirt and pulled her tray closer. Her mother was staring at her so intensely; she wondered what she was thinking.

"Harper, is everything all right? Is there

something I should know?" Yuna asked.

Taking another big bite so she wouldn't be able to speak, Harper shook her head. While she wanted to tell her mother everything, she didn't trust that her mother would believe her. After all, it was almost too much for Harper.

"If there is something, honey, I hope you will tell me," Yuna continued carefully. "I know that I haven't been there for you in the past when you needed me, but I'm here for you now and always. You can count on me, I promise."

Harper nodded, feeling guilty. Maybe she should tell her mother. But where would she even begin? Demons in the mirror? A witch after Kelly? Makeup that stole youth? It was all too much.

After her mother left, Harper pulled out a small notebook and began writing down everything that had happened so far. When she was done, she went onto her computer and began to research Jeune and Jenna, but she couldn't find much information. She'd have to wait for Dayo. Dayo could find anything on the internet.

As if she'd heard her name, Dayo texted her at that moment.

Dayo—Hey, u ok?

Harper—Yeah, lots to tell u

Dayo—is it bad?

Harper—Tell u later

Dayo—Ok see u

Harper—k

HOW TO STOP A WITCH

Tuesday afternoon

Anxious to see Dayo, Harper sat in the living room waiting for her to arrive from school. When the doorbell finally rang, she rushed to open it. Dayo took one look at Harper's face and let out a little scream of shock.

"What happened?"

Harper hurried Dayo up to her room before she explained.

"I touched the cameo," Harper explained. "Jenna is a witch who lived a long time ago. I think like back during the Salem witch trials period. She switched her soul into another woman's body and has been doing this for centuries. Which means she's probably killed hundreds of women! And her next target is Kelly!"

Dayo's mouth fell open and she sat gaping at Harper for a long moment.

"I know, it sounds unbelievable! But I watched it happen to the very first girl she put under her spell. And it has something to do with the cameo! It must be the way she's able to switch bodies with these young girls. I figured if I could hide the cameo, maybe Kelly would be safe. But when I went back to steal it, Kelly woke up and caught me in the act. And she hit me."

Harper could see that Dayo was so shocked she couldn't even talk.

Finally, Dayo shook her head in disbelief.

"So, we're not dealing with ghosts or demons, but a body-stealing witch?"

"Well, there is a demon that's working with her," Harper replied. "The one I saw in the mirror at Jeune. He helps Jenna collect all the stolen youth and turns it into beads. And I think Mrs. D said he acts as the security system for the shop."

"Okay, I guess that makes sense. Demon security. Definitely would stop people from breaking in!" Dayo responded. She was staring intently at Harper's face.

"But I can't believe your sister hit you hard

enough to give you a black eye! That's horrible! What the heck got into her? Did you tell your mom?"

"No, I told her it was an accident and I fell out of bed." Harper bit her lip. "It's not like Kelly to do this. Something has changed in her."

"Maybe she's already under the witch's spell!"

While the thought filled Harper's heart with painful dread, it was probably true. Otherwise, why would Kelly do something so violent? She and her sister may have fought before, but Kelly had never hurt her physically. Harper still couldn't believe it.

"So, what can we do to save her?" Dayo asked.

"I don't know," Harper admitted. "I'm waiting to hear back from my grandmother and Mrs. Devereux."

"But what do we do in the meantime?"

Harper grabbed her notebook and pen and looked hopefully at Dayo.

"I was hoping we could do some internet research," she said.

Rubbing her hands together and wiggling her fingers, Dayo said, "Let's do it!"

A few hours later, Harper was stunned at what Dayo was able to find.

"I don't know how you do it, Dayo," Harper said in amazement. "It's like magic."

Dayo laughed. "It's not magic; it's just looking for

information in different ways. For example, instead of just googling her name, we look for where else it might show up. While there were a few articles about her and Jeune, I found really helpful stuff in the company documents for Jeune. This article said Jeune is a subsidiary of this really old company called C. Wentworth, Inc., which was incorporated in 1792."

"What the heck is a subsidiary, and what does 'incorporated' mean?" Harper asked.

"Let me look it up," Dayo responded. "A subsidiary is a company owned by another company, which is the parent company. So C. Wentworth is the parent company of Jeune. And incorporated means to become a corporation."

"Hmmm, C. Wentworth," Harper mumbled. "That sounds really familiar."

"It's a perfume and soap company. See, they have a website," Dayo remarked. "Looks like fancy soaps."

"Wait a minute," Harper cut in. "C. Wentworth? In my dream, the witch's name was Constance Wentworth!"

Dayo's big brown eyes got even wider. "Then she must own the parent company also!"

"You said there's a website?"

"Yeah, but it didn't say anything much. However, I did find a wiki page!"

The girls leaned in close, their heads touching as they read the page.

"Whoa, that's a lot of history," Harper remarked.

"But it's fascinating!" Dayo was enthusiastic. "It started as an apothecary shop in New York City called W. J. Preston Apothecary and was run by Dr. William Preston and his wife, Prudence. The two were childless, and when Prudence died, Dr. Preston immediately remarried a much younger woman, Agatha Massey."

"Oh, that must have been the witch, taking over Agatha's body," Harper said.

Dayo shuddered. "And look, she did it again! Since Dr. Preston remained childless, he passed on ownership of the apothecary to his nephew, Matthew Preston, who was married to Christina Leary. He remarried twenty years later to a Laura Bennett. He also died childless, so the apothecary passed to his cousin, Gerard Preston. Gerard ran the shop with his wife, Claire, and then his adopted daughter, Angela. Does that mean Jenna was also Christina, Claire, and Angela?"

"Wow, that's so wrong! What happened after Angela?"

"It was bought by L. M. Gallagher in 1920, when

the company began making a popular cold cream."

"What's a cold cream?" Harper asked.

"That's like the stuff my grandma uses to wash her makeup off," Dayo replied.

"So, it's like a skin care product?"

Dayo nodded her head soberly. "Has she been stealing days from people for over a hundred years, since this cold cream was first invented?"

Harper rubbed her forehead. "I don't think so. I heard the demon say that this was a new project and that the youth beads were draining his powers."

"Well, that's good news, I guess?" Turning back to the computer, Dayo kept reading. "They also sell soaps and lotions. Their orange soda lotion is their most famous and best-selling product."

"Orange soda? I feel like I've smelled that a lot," Harper thought out loud. "I guess they are pretty successful."

"They have a manufacturing plant in Baltimore, Maryland. Jeune is their new line of makeup and skin care products under Jenna Graham's leadership. And Jenna is also listed as sole owner of C. Wentworth."

"She must be loaded," Harper said.

Dayo sat tapping her finger on the desk, lost in thought. Harper peered into her face, wondering what she was thinking. After a long moment, Dayo slammed her hands down, startling Harper.

"What is it, Dayo?"

"In your dream, Jenna said she'd been switching bodies every twenty years, for nearly four hundred years, right?"

"Yep."

"You know how much of a pain it must be for her to have to change ownership every twenty years?"

"Yeah, she was definitely not happy about it."

"But why would she think Kelly is going to fix all that?"

This had puzzled Harper also. What was so special about Kelly that made Jenna think her problems would be solved?

"I don't know."

Dayo was staring intently at Harper. "And that's what's bothering me. I feel like we're missing something."

"Maybe we can talk to Grandma together," Harper said.

"Me too?" Dayo asked in surprise.

"Yeah, you're, like, the smartest person I know. And I'm so grateful for all your help."

With a big smile, Dayo grabbed Harper's hands and held them tightly. "That's what best friends do."

Looking down at their clasped hands, Harper got teary-eyed. "But I feel bad. All you do is help me and feed me, and I've put you in danger and now you can see ghosts. I'm a terrible friend."

Dayo started laughing. "First of all, coming and eating my mom's cooking is a huge favor for me. Do you remember that I'm an only child? She is trying to stuff me full like a turkey all the time!"

Dayo puffed out her cheeks, making Harper smile. Dayo's mom did love to taste test her recipes on Harper. And she liked that Harper never turned down anything she made.

"Second, I've always felt a little lonely, but now I'm not. And I love your family, even Kelly. So we have to save her."

"Thank you, best friend." Harper hugged Dayo hard.

"You're welcome, best friend."

Suddenly, Harper's stomach gurgled loudly, causing them to both giggle.

"That reminds me, I'm supposed to bring you over for dinner. My mom had an event today, and she has a lot of leftovers. Please take some or I'll be eating it frozen for months!"

"Let's go now!" Harper jumped to her feet. "And then we can call my grandma."

On the way downstairs, they ran into Kelly coming home.

"Ew, what happened to your eye?" Kelly asked.

"You don't remember?" Harper asked.

Kelly looked affronted. "Why would I remember? Seriously, are you feeling okay?"

"I'm fine," Harper said. "Going to Dayo's."

Once outside, Harper could not contain her disbelief.

"Can you believe the nerve of her, to pretend that she didn't hit me?" Harper fumed.

But Dayo looked thoughtful. "I don't think she was pretending," she said. "She honestly doesn't remember."

Harper frowned. "You really think so?"

"I'm positive," Dayo replied. "She was shocked when she saw you and then offended that you would think she would know anything. I don't think she was acting."

"Well, she is a terrible actor," Harper mused. "You really think she doesn't remember?"

"I'm positive." Dayo grabbed Harper's arm and started walking. "But if she can't remember, then do you think she was under a spell or something when she hit you?"

"I don't know. We're just going to have to ask my grandma," Harper said.

At Dayo's house, Harper's black eye caused alarmed concern from Mrs. Clayton, as well as a slice of hot blackberry pie with vanilla ice cream. As she was eating, Dayo's dad came home early and did a double take at seeing her.

"So, who won?" he asked.

Harper dipped her head in embarrassment. "It was an accident," she said meekly. "I fell out of bed."

"Mm-hm." Dr. Clayton sat down at the table, folded his hands, and looked at her quietly.

"Now, Harper, I have seen a lot of black eyes in my life, and I would bet my medical license that it was no accident." His eyes were kind. "Is there something going on that you might need adult help with but are afraid to ask for?"

Harper and Dayo traded glances. Dayo's dad was an ER doctor, so there wasn't a medical problem he hadn't seen. Besides, she didn't want to lie to him.

"Please don't tell my parents?" Harper asked.

"It depends on what you tell me, honey," Dr. Clayton responded. "If you trust me, you know that I will only ever do what is in your best interest."

Harper nodded. "It's just that I don't want you to think badly of Kelly. She didn't seem like herself when she hit me."

"Yes, Daddy! She didn't even remember she did it!" Dayo said.

Dr. Clayton stood up and came around the table. "Okay, Harper, I won't say anything to your parents as long as you let me take a closer look at it."

After a thorough examination, he was finally satisfied that she was actually fine. "Doesn't look like you have any fractures, so I think ice tonight and warm compresses in the morning will help. Take some pain medications if it hurts, but no aspirin. And you let me know if anything changes, okay?"

Since dinner was still an hour away, the girls went upstairs to call Harper's grandmother.

"Harper! Is everything all right?"

"Yes, I'm at Dayo's house, and we were wondering if Mrs. D could come visit us here," Harper said.

"I'm here, dear child."

Harper jumped, and Dayo let out a tiny scream.

"Harper, I see her! I can see Mrs. Devereux," Dayo whispered.

The spirit guide bowed at Dayo, resplendent in an aquamarine dress that shimmered with her every movement.

"Wow, she's gorgeous," Dayo said. She stood up and gave the ghost a deep bow.

"I like your friend, Harper," Mrs. Devereux said with a little smile. "She has a beautiful aura and is destined to do great things."

"Well, I know that!" Harper agreed. She could see how embarrassed but pleased her friend was to hear this.

"How long have you been able to see us, dear?" Mrs. Devereux asked.

"Since Raku Island," Dayo answered shyly.

"Ah yes, that would explain it," Mrs. Devereux remarked. "Being around so much spiritual energy must have fully opened your channels."

Mrs. Devereux turned to Harper. "But now that your friend can see spirits, it would be best for you to provide her with some of your grandmother's protective charm pouches."

"Oh, right," Harper agreed. At Dayo's questioning glance, Harper explained, "They'll protect you so that your bedroom will always be safe from unwanted spirits."

"Harper, why don't you put me on speaker?" Grandma Lee said loudly through the phone.

Once on speaker, Grandma Lee asked about Kelly. She wasn't surprised to learn that Kelly had no memory of hitting Harper.

"She is under the spell of that cursed object," Grandma Lee said.

"Cursed object? You mean the cameo?"

"Yes, it was the object that the witch used to steal her first victim's body. She has continued to use it for centuries to do great evil," Mrs. Devereux explained. "Just having it in her possession gives the witch control over Kelly."

"So let me steal it, and we'll smash it!"

"No good," Mrs. Devereux replied. "The only way to do that would be to destroy the witch who created it."

Harper slouched, deflated.

"So what do we do? How do we save Kelly?"

"You have to stop this witch once and for all, by attacking her when she's most vulnerable," Mrs. Devereux said.

"When is that?"

"When she is attempting to switch bodies."

Dayo gasped in alarm. "But won't that be too late?" she asked, looking back and forth from Mrs. Devereux to Harper. "What if she's already switched with Kelly before we're able to act?"

"Grandma, that's too dangerous!" Harper exploded. "We have to do something before she tries to switch. We can't risk Kelly's life!"

"We can't risk your life, either, Harper!" Grandmother Lee said. "We've tried to see what other options there were, but she is too powerful and dangerous for a young girl like you to take on. I wish I could be there with you! This is the only way you'll even have a chance to get close enough to stop her."

"But what about Kelly . . . ?" As Harper deflated, Dayo put an arm around her in comfort.

Mrs. Devereux floated close to both of them. "Harper, your grandmother is very upset about this. She has been reaching out to other shamans to see if any will help, but they are all too afraid. We must stop this witch, and this is the only good chance we have."

"So what do I do?"

"The night of the transfer, you and your friends must disrupt the spell and protect Kelly by placing a mirror between them, at just the right moment."

"When is that?"

"It is when the spell is at its strongest, and there is no turning back. The souls will start to separate from their physical forms. At that moment, if you place a mirror between them facing the witch, the witch's soul will then become trapped in the mirror and can be destroyed. But it must be at that moment only."

"How will I know when that is? And what about

Kelly? Won't she be trapped also?"

"As long as you face the mirror to the witch only, Kelly's soul will just return to her own body. But you must watch the witch's eyes carefully. When her soul is ready to transfer, her eyes will change from green to black. Only then can you trap her."

It all sounded terribly risky. If she made any mistake, Kelly would be switched into Jenna's body.

"But if something happens and I'm unable to stop the switch, then Kelly will have to live in Jenna's body forever?"

There was a long silence. "I'm sorry to tell you this, but because the physical form of Jenna is not the witch's true form, it exists solely because of her magic. Without it, the body will rapidly deteriorate."

Dayo covered her mouth in horror, and Harper could not help but shudder. "So that means Kelly would die," she whispered.

"But I have faith in you, Harper. I know you can save her," Grandma said firmly. "However, we don't have much time. There are only three nights before the full moon, and you're going to have to ask your friends for help."

"You mean Dayo?"

"Yes, and your cousin Leo."

Harper was surprised. "Leo? Why him?"

"Because he can see spirits now. He will be of great help to you."

Harper pulled a face. "He's kind of a chicken, so I don't know how helpful he would be."

"Any help would be good, Harper," Dayo interrupted. "It's not just for Kelly's sake. I'm worried about you, too."

"Not only is your friend smart, but she is right," Mrs. Devereux remarked. "There is a power in three that will be very useful to you. And you will need all the help you can get. You are going up against a powerful witch."

"Okay," Harper agreed.

"Good girl," her grandmother said. "You must teach Dayo and Leo how to use your bells."

"Will they work on a witch?" Harper asked.

"They might not be enough," Grandma replied in a troubled voice. "But they will work on the demon and keep him from helping her. In fact, I believe the demon is there to protect the witch while she is in her most vulnerable state."

Harper frowned. "If the bells work on a demon, why wouldn't they work on a witch? They killed the demon monsters on Razu Island, and they were a lot scarier than a witch."

"Never underestimate the power of a witch,

especially as ancient and evil as this one," Mrs. Devereux said sharply.

"Remember, Harper, it was the souls who helped you destroy the Razu. You could not have done it alone," her grandmother reminded her.

Chastised, Harper bit her lip. The Razu were soul eaters. Their bellies had been filled with all the spirits of people they'd killed over hundreds of years. She'd called on the souls within the monsters to burst out. That's what had destroyed them. The sheer strength in numbers of thousands of souls eager to break free of their prison.

Her grandmother was right. This situation was completely different. So what was Harper supposed to do? How could she defeat an evil witch?

"I'm scared," Harper admitted. "I wish you were here with me, Grandma."

Dayo reached over and patted Harper's back. "I'll help you."

"And so will I," Mrs. Devereux said. "But remember, Harper, you are also extremely powerful. In some ways, even more so than this witch."

"How's that?"

"Your power comes from inside. It is part of who you are," Mrs. Devereux said. "The witch relies on dark magic and a demon. Her power is not her own."

Harper didn't understand what this meant. "So how do I beat her?"

This time it was Grandma Lee who spoke up. "Harper, you must concentrate on the flow of your energy as it relates to the world around you. That is your power. When the souls helped you destroy the Razu, they opened up your spiritual channels so that you could direct the energy and let it flow through you."

"But that was because there were thousands of spirits around me!"

"There is energy everywhere! It surrounds you. You must control it and harness it. And then you can direct it like a weapon."

"But I have no idea how," Harper complained.

"That is why we will train tonight."

UNDER THE WITCH'S SPELL

Dayo's mom fed Harper a delicious dinner of roast chicken, greens, and mashed potatoes. She then sent her home with an aluminum tray of food. After giving effusive thanks, Harper put on her coat, and Dayo walked her to the door. "I wish I could sleep over, but you know how my parents are about school nights," Dayo sighed.

"It's okay. I'll FaceTime you later."

After a big hug, Harper quickly walked the few blocks home. Entering her house, Harper yelled, "Yummy food is here!" and went to set it on the dining table. Yuna's face lit up to see the tray of food and immediately called Dayo's mom to thank her.

But it was Michael who was the happiest.

"Oh, boy! I love Dayo's mom's food the bestest!"

Harper opened up the tray, and Michael clapped his hands in joy.

"Chicken! My favorite!"

"I thought pizza was your favorite?" Harper teased.

"Wait, he told me hamburgers were his favorite," Leo chimed in.

"Right now, this chicken is my favorite!" Michael insisted.

Laughing, Leo leaned over to take a whiff and smiled broadly. "That smells amazing!"

"And it's all yours. I ate at Dayo's."

Yuna got off the phone and brought over plates and silverware.

"Harper, your timing was perfect," she said. "Your dad is going to be really late tonight, and I was just trying to figure out what to order for dinner.

"All right, everyone, go wash up. Harper, can you tell your sister to come eat?"

Harper walked upstairs and knocked on her sister's door. There was no response. She knocked harder and called Kelly's name loudly. Still no response. Harper opened the door, walked in, and found her sister sitting at her desk staring into a lighted makeup mirror. She was wearing the cameo and caressing it as she stared at her reflection.

"Kelly," Harper said loudly. "Mom wants you to come down for dinner."

"I'm not hungry," Kelly replied in a weird, dazed-sounding voice that was totally not like her.

"Mom's gonna be mad," Harper said. Suddenly, very afraid for her sister, she tugged at Kelly's arm. "Come on, let's go."

Kelly whipped her arm away so hard Harper nearly fell. "I said no."

Her eyes glared at Harper with a coldness that she'd never seen before. This was definitely not her sister acting like this. She backed out and ran downstairs to tell her mother.

"Mom, Kelly refuses to come down. She is just sitting there staring at that cameo necklace her weirdo boss gave her."

A mix of anger and concern crossed Yuna's face. "I'm so upset with that Jeune owner," she muttered. "I am going to have to go talk to her. Who gives a seventeen-year-old girl an expensive antique necklace?"

Harper followed her mother upstairs and watched as Yuna forced Kelly to come downstairs. Something about Yuna's stern, no-nonsense approach seemed to snap Kelly out of her malaise.

"Take off that cameo, Kelly," her mother insisted. "There's no reason to wear it around the house. It's extremely expensive and you shouldn't even have it."

Kelly's hands tightened reflexively around the cameo. "But it's mine! It was a gift!"

"Fine, but it stays up here in your room. It's too valuable to wear around every day."

Almost against her will, Kelly took off the necklace. As soon as she put it down on the dresser, she changed dramatically.

"What's for dinner?" she asked in her normal voice. "I'm starved!"

As she walked toward the door, she turned back to glare at Harper.

"Don't you dare touch it, Harper."

Harper threw up her hands. "I wasn't going to!"

"Come on, honey, let's go downstairs," Yuna interjected. She gestured for Harper to leave.

"Mom, I ate already," Harper reminded her.

Taking one last look at the cameo, Harper walked past her glaring sister and went straight to her room. Locking the door, she video-called her grandmother.

"Harper, I know it's cold outside, but can you meet Mrs. Devereux in your backyard?"

"Now?"

"Yes, she wants you to work on your powers outside."

Sneaking back downstairs, she saw her family at the dinner table. She grabbed her heavy coat from the closet and went through the kitchen and out the side door to the backyard. The air was so cold that every breath Harper let out was a big cloud of white smoke. Shivering, she buttoned up her coat and waited.

"Harper, I am here, but I am not going to materialize in front of you tonight. I want your entire focus solely on your training."

"Yes, ma'am."

"Do you see the pile of chopped wood in the corner? I want you to pick up a log."

Harper concentrated on moving one log. It was bigger than anything she'd tried yet but not too terribly heavy. And still she struggled with it.

"I can't."

"This is life and death, child. There is no giving up allowed."

Mrs. D's words chilled Harper. Reminding herself that Kelly was in terrible danger, Harper focused on the log again. She reminded herself she was not moving the log but the energy around it. And energy was not heavy. Suddenly, the log floated up and moved across the yard.

"Very good, Harper. Now throw it."

To throw it, she needed speed. She needed a whip-like action, or a spring. She imagined all the energy surrounding the log coming together and twisting, turning, and coiling around it. Concentrating on the ever-tightening energy, Harper released it and watched as the log whipped across the yard and landed with a loud thud.

"You're doing really well, dear child. Now do two at a time."

After nearly thirty minutes of practicing, Harper was able to move several logs at once and even send them flying in different directions.

"Excellent work. Remember, your mind is your most powerful weapon."

Now knowing what she was capable of, Harper felt less afraid of having to face the witch.

"That's enough for tonight. Go on in and warm up."

Relieved, Harper ran back into the warmth of the house only to hear Kelly yelling at their mom.

"I will not quit!"

"Kelly, this is nonnegotiable. You will not be

returning to that store."

"You can't stop me." Kelly's voice was cold and flat.

"Don't test me, Kelly. You will not be happy."

"No, you'll be sorry, Mom! Don't threaten me or I will leave home and you'll never see me again!"

Kelly pushed her chair back so hard it toppled over, and she stormed away. Everyone remained frozen in their seats. Even Michael was quiet with alarm.

"Mom?" Harper called out. "Are you okay?"

Yuna shook her head. "I don't know what has gotten into her. There's something very wrong. Harper, do you know?"

"It's the makeup," Michael said loudly. "It's poison. She has to stop using it."

Yuna turned to look at Harper. "It isn't a ghost? You would tell me, right, Harper?"

Nodding her head slowly, Harper said, "It isn't a ghost, Mom."

But how could she tell her it was a witch trying to steal her sister's body? Maybe it would be better coming from Grandma. She looked at the hurt and concern on her mother's face and didn't want to worry her any more. And what could she do anyway? Her mom would have no idea what to do. The truth was, there was nothing her mom could do to help Kelly. It would be better not to tell her.

"Mom, why don't you read some books to Michael? Leo and I will clean up," Harper said.

"Great idea, Harper!" Michael crowed. Jumping down from his seat, he grabbed Yuna by the hand and led her out of the dining room, chattering happily about what books to read.

Leo and Harper cleared the table and loaded up the dishwasher.

"Seriously, your sister is getting out of control," Leo said.

"She can't help herself," Harper responded. "She's under the spell of that cameo."

"Let's get rid of it tonight."

Harper shook her head. "The only way is to destroy the witch."

Startled by her words, Leo shuddered violently. "You have to kill her?"

His words gave Harper great pause. "Kill" was such a terrible word. Though Jenna was an evil witch, she was still a human, right? It wasn't like getting rid of a bad spirit or a scary demon monster. This was a person.

"I—I can't do that," Harper stuttered.

"Then what? How do you save Kelly?"

Harper took a deep breath. "I'm going to need your help."

"Who, me?" he asked in surprise. He was quiet for so long that Harper was about to explain that it was Grandma Lee's idea, when he finally responded.

"Okay, I'll do it."

Harper blinked in surprise. "Just like that? Without asking me what's involved?"

Closing the dishwasher, Leo faced her. "You and Dayo helped me and saved all those people on Razu Island. Neither of you hesitated. You just did the right thing. Kelly's my cousin, and I'm older than you. Of course I have to help you save her. Whatever it takes."

"Well, I don't know what being barely a year older than me has to do with it, but thank you," Harper responded.

"So, what do I have to do?"

"You and Dayo have to learn how to use my bells after school tomorrow."

"Cool. I'm excited."

"Really?" Harper asked.

"Actually, more like terrified."

HARPER'S POWERS
Wednesday afternoon

After school, Dayo, Leo, and Harper all met up in front of the building to ride home together. Dayo was bouncing with excitement while Leo was quieter than usual. As they rode, Leo biked ahead of them.

"I think a hundred people must have asked me about my eye today," Harper groused. "And everyone's a comedian."

"It does look pretty bad," Dayo said sympathetically. "It's kind of a glorious shade of purple. But wait until it turns greenish yellow."

"I'll be hideous."

They both laughed.

"Hey, are we stopping by to pick up Michael today?" Dayo asked.

Harper shook her head. "He has tae kwon do."

"My cousin's an orange belt at Master Park's Dojang," Dayo said. "He really loves it there."

"So does Michael," Harper said. "And he's so cute when he practices his forms."

As they chatted, they were nearing the one large intersection they had to cross to get home. They had the crosswalk light, and Leo was already halfway through the intersection when they heard the sudden blaring of a truck. It skidded through the red light and was screeching toward Leo. Harper screamed, "No!" Throwing out her hand, she pushed Leo and his bike out of the truck's path, just as it passed in front of them. The truck finally skidded to a stop several feet away, but Harper could see Leo sitting on the sidewalk across the street, a dazed expression on his face.

Harper and Dayo rushed across as the truck driver came running to Leo's side.

"Hey, kid, are you all right?" He helped pull Leo to his feet.

Leo nodded numbly.

"My brakes locked up, and I lost control," the truck driver was explaining. "I was so scared I was going to hit you! But, man, I've never seen anyone move so fast!" The truck driver let out a relieved sigh. After checking on Leo one more time, the driver went back to his vehicle.

"Leo, are you sure you're okay?" Harper asked.

Leo nodded again.

"I almost had a heart attack!" Dayo exclaimed, patting her chest. "I thought for sure you were gonna get hit."

"So did I," Leo muttered. He stared at Harper with an odd expression. "I had the strangest feeling, like somebody shoved me out of the way."

At his words, Dayo turned and looked at Harper with a gasp. "Harper, I saw you throw your arm out right before Leo went flying. Did you do that?"

Nervous that they would be overheard, Harper got back on her bike. "Come on, let's talk in private," she said softly.

"Harper, it was you!" Dayo shout-whispered.

Speeding away on her bike, Harper led the way home. Dayo and Leo waited until they were in the house before they began bombarding her with questions.

"I thought you could only move small things," Dayo said. "How were you able to move Leo?"

Leo was shaking his head. "There's no way Harper did that."

"She can do it! I've seen her move things."

"It's impossible!"

"Leo, we both can see ghosts now," Dayo asserted. "Nothing's impossible."

This shut him up, and they both turned to stare at Harper.

"I'm hungry," Harper said. Entering the kitchen, she opened the pantry as the others crowded around her. "Excuse me, a little personal space, please."

Leo backed off, but Dayo stayed right by Harper's side, grinning like the Cheshire cat from the *Alice in Wonderland* movie.

"I know it was you." Dayo poked at her. "But I thought you couldn't move anything that big. You've been practicing, haven't you?"

Harper ignored her, pulling bags of chips and cookies aside as she hunted for Korean snacks.

"Come on, just show Leo what you can do," Dayo said. "Please?"

Without responding, Harper stepped aside and floated all the packages of snack food out onto the kitchen table.

"No way!" Leo yelled in disbelief while Dayo jumped and clapped in delight.

"How the heck is this even possible?" Leo asked.

Harper scratched her head, trying to figure out how to explain it.

"You know how ghosts can move things around sometimes?" Harper asked.

Leo nodded.

"Well, so yeah, it's like that."

Both Leo and Dayo looked confused.

"I don't get it," Dayo said. "You're not a ghost."

"But I can channel the same spiritual energy to move things."

"That . . . is . . . so . . . cool." Dayo was bouncing up and down. "Can you lift me up?"

Dayo shrieked when Harper used her powers to float Dayo gently in the air while spinning her slowly. After she put her down, she looked at her cousin, who flung his hands out, as if to ward Harper off.

"Don't you dare!"

Grinning, Harper focused on Leo's hoodie, pulling the hood all the way over his face and tightening the strings, so that all they could see was his nose poking out of the small hole. Dayo burst into laughter as Leo tried to untie himself.

"Ha-ha, very funny, Harper. Now cut it out."

Freeing her cousin of his hood, Harper sat down and opened a bag of chocolate churro snacks. Dayo sat next to her, and they both began to scarf down the sweet bite-sized chocolate pieces with a hint of cinnamon.

Leo shook his head. "It might have been better if they weren't called churros. Because it isn't an authentic churro."

The girls looked at the little square treats for a moment and then continued to eat them.

"But they are delicious," Harper said.

"Mm-hmm, ever since your mom gave us a few bags, my mom's been going to the Korean mart to get them every week," Dayo said. "My dad is addicted to them."

"Me too," Harper replied. She looked at a churro chip and said, "While you can never replace the absolute goodness of a real churro, we still love you so much."

"Okay. When you finish stuffing your face, let's get to training," Leo cut in. "I admit, I'm getting nervous."

At his words, Harper jumped to her feet, wiped her fingers on her jeans, and told them she'd be right back. She ran up to her room and grabbed her messenger bag with her shaman bells and bowls. She then found two charm pouches and went downstairs. Calling Leo and Dayo to the living room, she set up her bowls and bells on the floor in front of the fireplace.

"These bells are Wisdom and Truth," Harper said. "Wisdom opens up the spiritual pathways and Truth reveals all that's hidden." Wisdom was slightly narrower than Truth, which had a wider bell. Harper handed Wisdom to Leo and Truth to Dayo. "When you ring these bells and if you use the right words, they will immobilize evil spirits. With Wisdom you must say, 'Through the power of the Ancient One, I bind you. You will do no harm.' When you ring Truth you must say, 'Through the power of the Worthy One, I bind you. You will do no harm.'"

Leo's brows were furrowed, but Dayo was nodding enthusiastically.

"We should have a salt ring around us, right, Harper?" Dayo asked.

Harper slapped herself on the head. "Why do I always forget that?"

"Isn't salt just a superstition thing?" Leo asked dubiously.

"It works," Dayo replied with a no-nonsense look. "It will protect us from the demon."

Hiding her grin, Harper proceeded to walk them through the basics of using the bells and the bowls to bind the demon and destroy it. They practiced for an hour and discussed what they would have to do the day of the full moon. It was clear that while Dayo was committed and enthusiastic, Leo still had some skepticism he couldn't quite shake. But as she explained what they would have to do to stop the witch, both of their moods became more serious. They were all aware of the risks involved.

Harper suddenly felt an overwhelming dread. If she messed up, not only would she be in danger, but Dayo and Leo would also. There was so much at stake.

"Maybe you shouldn't do this," Harper said.

"What? Why would you say that, Harper?" Dayo asked.

"This is really dangerous. I don't want anything to happen to you guys."

Dayo moved over to Harper's side and gave her a big hug. "Listen, you: As long as Leo and I help, everything is going to be fine, okay?"

"Yeah, I would be more worried if you tried to do this yourself, Harper," Leo said. "But the three of us together is going to be safer."

Tears pricked at Harper's eyes, and she swiped at them with the backs of her hands. For so long, she'd felt terribly alone with her fear. To have a best friend who believed in her and a cousin who was willing to help her, despite the danger, made Harper finally feel a powerful sense of belonging.

"Thank you, guys," she said in a raspy voice. "I just wish there was something I could do to make sure you both were protected."

At that moment, the doorbell rang. Harper went to answer it and greeted the mailman, who had an overnight package that needed a signature. Signing for it, she immediately saw that it was from her grandmother.

"Guys, my grandma just sent me something. Must be important to mail overnight."

Sitting back down on the floor, she opened the package to find a letter and four small red envelopes with gold lettering on the outside, in what looked like Chinese characters.

> *Dear Harper,*
>
> *I am once again not close enough to help you through this very difficult and dangerous time. I am so sorry about that. I've also been worried about Dayo and Leo. They are not spirit hunters by blood, which means that they are putting themselves in danger to help Kelly. And while I know you will protect them, I wanted to give them extra protection. I have made these special bujeok to ward off evil for*

all of you and Kelly. Your mother never let me make
them for you before, but now I think she will accept
them. All three of you must carry the bujeok with
you at all times. Try to get Kelly to do so also, even
if you have to sneak it into her wallet. It will help.
And please be careful.

> *Love,*
> *Grandma*

Harper carefully opened one of the red envelopes and found a small folded yellow paper. It unfolded into a rectangular sheet, and on the sheet was a drawing of a strange figure with unusual markings in bright red ink. Harper let out a big sigh of relief.

"This is exactly what we needed. Thank you, Grandma!"

"What is it?" Dayo asked.

"It's a bujeok, like a protective talisman," Harper replied. "I've seen them all over Grandma's shrine room. This one is specific for keeping evil away. She also makes lots of other kinds for people. For luck, health, fortune, you know."

"Oh, I would want all of those also!" Dayo exclaimed.

"It's just a paper charm," Leo scoffed. "They don't actually work."

Raising an eyebrow, Harper replied, "Okay, then, I won't give you yours."

Leo reached over and snatched a red envelope out of her hand.

"I didn't say I wouldn't take one." He put it in his pocket. "I mean, it can't hurt."

They all laughed, but Harper was relieved to know that her best friend and her cousin would not be going unprotected. She had a lot of faith in her grandmother's shaman powers. The bujeok would protect them. And so would she.

PROTECTING KELLY

Wednesday night

Later that night, after training with Mrs. Devereux on her telekinesis, Harper tried to figure out where she could put the bujeok for Kelly. She could put the talisman in Kelly's wallet, but she knew that when Kelly was at work, she kept her bag in a locker in the back room. That meant she wouldn't have her wallet on her while working. So, what was the one thing that Kelly always kept on her?

"Her cell phone!"

Of course! Kelly always carried her cell phone everywhere. She even took it into the bathroom with her, which Harper thought was gross, but apparently this was something all teenagers did. If she could get her hands on it, that would be perfect. Kelly's phone had a fancy new flower case cover. Harper could slip the bujeok inside the case, and Kelly would never even know it was there. Harper felt relieved. This was a good plan. The bujeok would keep Kelly safe. At least until the full moon.

Then a loud noise from downstairs startled her.

"Kelly, do not disrespect your mother!"

Harper was shocked to hear her father yelling. He was the calm one in the family and almost never lost his temper. She stepped out into the hallway and looked over the railing. A little hand slipped into hers.

"Michael, shouldn't you be in bed?"

"I can't sleep. Too noisy," Michael whispered. "Why is Kelly being so mean?"

Harper tightened her hand on his as they listened to the fight happening downstairs.

"I'm seventeen years old. I have a job, and I can take care of myself," Kelly yelled. "Don't tell me what to do or I will leave and never come back!"

"You threatened this before, young lady. You are still a minor and our responsibility!"

"I don't have to be! Jenna would gladly have me live with her! She says you're both too controlling!"

"Well, you can't live with her because you are our daughter and our dependent," her mother replied.

"I can emancipate myself! Jenna said so!"

"That's it. We need to go and talk with this Jenna person," Peter responded. "How dare she say this nonsense to our daughter?!"

"Don't you dare! You will embarrass me!"

"You can go with us!"

"I will not!"

"Right now, Kelly! This behavior is going to end today!"

Harper and Michael tiptoed down the stairs to see their parents pulling a loud, complaining Kelly out of the house.

As the door slammed, Leo came cautiously out of his room.

"Is Kelly going to be okay?" Michael asked.

Harper picked up her little brother and gave him a squeeze. "Yes, she's going to be fine. Just a few more days, and I promise she'll be back to normal."

Over Michael's shoulder, Leo and Harper nodded to each other. They would save Kelly.

An hour later, Harper's parents and Kelly returned home. Kelly entered the house screaming, "I hate you!" She ran up to her room and slammed her door.

Harper went down and found her parents sitting

at the kitchen table, both looking very upset. She listened as they comforted each other.

"Well, at least she seemed reasonable," her father was saying.

"No, she's not!" Yuna cut in. "She should have agreed to release her immediately, instead of insisting she see the week out."

"Honey, it's just a few more days, and she won't go back."

"But to have Kelly work until midnight on Friday is ridiculous! I'm still angry at you for agreeing!"

"She said the weekends are very busy in the shop. I thought it was a reasonable request," Peter soothed.

Harper quietly returned to her room. That was clever of Jenna. She needed Kelly to come to work on Friday night, so she'd gotten her parents to agree. Harper opened up the remaining red envelope containing the bujeok. It was already folded small and thin enough to fit inside Kelly's phone case. She would have to do it tonight when Kelly was asleep.

Unable to sleep, Harper practiced all her training until three a.m., when she felt it was safe to enter Kelly's room. Opening the door to her sister's room, she was stunned to see Kelly sitting in front of her vanity, staring motionlessly at her reflection in the mirror. As Harper entered, she looked into the mirror and was shocked to find the red eyes of the demon in Kelly's reflection. Quickly, Harper unfolded the bujeok and held it up to the mirror. The demon disappeared immediately, and Kelly collapsed in her chair. Harper sighed in relief.

"Kelly, are you all right?" Harper asked.

Kelly mumbled something incoherently, her eyes closing. Helping her sister to the bed, Harper tucked her in and watched her fall asleep. Only then did she grab Kelly's phone from the bedside table. Taking off the phone case, she carefully folded up the bujeok and placed it between the phone and the case and closed it tightly again. Sitting next to Kelly, she noted the unhealthy pallor of her normally vibrant sister's face. A chill went down her spine. Why was the demon in the mirror? Her grandmother had put protective spells all around the house. How had he been able to breach the defenses? Unless Kelly had unintentionally let him in.

That had to be the answer. An evil creature could only come to their house if they were invited. Ever since working at Jeune, Kelly had not been herself, as if she was under a spell. She must have unknowingly let the demon follow her home. But how could Harper stop Kelly from doing it again? This was really unnerving. The demon knew where she lived. She could only hope that the bujeok was enough for now.

"I'm going to protect you, Kelly, no matter what," Harper whispered. "I promise."

A WARNING

Thursday morning

Harper had spent four hours in bed awake and worried about all that had transpired in Kelly's room. Exhausted and concerned was a bad combination. When her alarm rang, she got up and went immediately to Kelly's door and knocked.

"What?" Kelly yelled.

Taking that as an invitation, Harper opened the door and saw Kelly ready to leave for school.

"What do you want?" Kelly's voice was hostile.

"So last night, did you hear or see anything weird?" Harper asked.

"Like what?"

"I don't know, something scary?"

Kelly rolled her eyes. "The only scary thing I've seen is your face. Seriously, what is wrong with your eye? It's gross."

Kelly picked up her schoolbag and pushed Harper out of her room. "I'm leaving. I can't stand being in this house anymore."

Watching her sister walk out of the house and into her friend's waiting car, Harper was disturbed to realize Kelly really had no recollection of what had happened the night before. Just like when she'd hit her that night she'd touched the cameo. It was as if Kelly's memory had been wiped clean or she was under a trance. This had to be the demon's doing. But why? What was the purpose of all this?

"Harper, it rained last night, and the roads are icy. You and Leo can't ride your bikes to school!" her mother yelled up to her from the living room.

"Okay!" Harper yelled back.

Just then she got a text from Dayo.

Dayo—Mom said we have to walk.

Harper—Mine too! Meet you in fifteen?

Dayo—Ok

Rushing through her morning routine, Harper dressed and ran downstairs to eat a quick bowl of cereal. Michael and Leo were sitting at the table eating toaster waffles.

"Honey, you don't want anything warm instead?" her mother asked. She was dressed in a pantsuit and drinking coffee.

Harper shook her head as she crunched on a large spoonful of cornflakes.

"I'm afraid I'll need you and Leo to watch Michael for me tonight and tomorrow night," her mother sighed. "Your dad and I are on a very important case, and we will probably be working all weekend. And Kelly is working late on Friday night."

Harper and Leo glanced at each other in dismay. They'd planned to sneak out when Harper's parents went to bed. There was no way she wanted to bring her baby brother to an evil witch's house.

"Oh, bummer, we were all going to go hang out at a friend's house tomorrow night. Dayo and I were even going to drag Leo with us. You know how hard it's been for him to make friends here."

Her mom looked at them in surprise. "Why am I only hearing about it now?"

"Because I've been trying to get Leo to go all week and finally got him to say yes, right, Leo?"

"Er, yeah, I didn't really want to go, but Harper's been twisting my arm . . . ," Leo answered, and glared at Harper.

"Who is it? I should call their parents . . ."

"Mom! We're in middle school! That would humiliate us!"

"Well, I have to know whose house you'll be at," Yuna said mildly.

Harper thought frantically and then remembered hearing that some of her friends really were hanging out this Friday.

"Devon Marcus," she said. "He's like the most popular kid in school. It's gonna be Dayo and Judy, Maya, Tyler, Gabby, and a bunch of Devon's soccer friends."

Yuna gave them both a big smile. "Harper, this will be the first get-together you're going to!"

"Yay," Harper said. Internally she groaned. This meant that they'd really have to go.

"Great! I'll find a babysitter for tomorrow, and you guys have a good time! Remember curfew is midnight!"

"That's fine!" Harper said in relief. If all went well, they would be home right on time.

"Aw nuts," Michael complained. "I don't want to have a babysitter. I want to go with you guys."

Harper leaned over to ruffle his hair. "You would be so bored. I promise to make it up to you, okay?"

"Anything I want?" Michael asked eagerly.

"As long as it doesn't cost too much, then it's a deal!"

Harper and Leo walked over to Dayo's house to pick her up on the way to school. As they approached her gate, Dayo stepped out of her front door.

"I couldn't sleep at all last night! I was so nervous," Dayo said.

"Me neither," Leo admitted.

"I guess we all had a bad night," Harper agreed.

"But I'm so glad your grandmother sent us those protective paper charms, Harper. I have to admit they do make me feel better."

"Me too," Harper replied. There was too much danger, and Harper couldn't stop worrying about what would happen to them. Just knowing that her friends had some protection was a small relief.

Dayo linked arms with Harper so they could walk together.

"Were you able to put one in a safe spot for Kelly?" Dayo asked.

Harper nodded. "I figured the one thing in the world that Kelly always has on her is her phone, so I slipped it between her phone and her phone case."

This made both Dayo and Leo laugh. A cold wind blasted them as they turned the corner, making them huddle together a little more closely.

The chill reminded Harper of Kelly, the demon, and her dream. As she relayed it all to Dayo and Leo, they all took on a frightened seriousness.

"So how did the demon find you if your house is supposed to be protected?" Dayo asked.

Harper had wondered the same thing. "It has to be Kelly," Harper replied. "She invited him in."

"Why would she do that?" Leo asked in shock.

"It's not like she would do it on purpose," Harper answered. "She was in a trance. She doesn't even know what she's doing. That's the problem."

"And now he knows who you are, Harper."

They were all quiet as they walked.

"Did you tell your grandma?" Leo asked.

"No, and don't tell her or Mrs. D," Harper warned. "I don't want them to worry. I think the important thing is that I have to be extra careful."

Dayo hugged Harper's arm tight in concern.

"Oh, there's one more thing," Harper said. "We're going to have to go to Devon's house tomorrow night for a little bit."

"But you hate parties! And we don't have a

birthday present!" Dayo exclaimed.

"So that's what the get-together was for!" Harper smacked her head in chagrin. "Ow! My eye."

Leo snickered. Shooting him a dirty look, Harper patted Dayo's arm.

"Don't worry, we can raid my mom's stationery drawer. She always keeps a bunch of gift cards for emergency presents."

"That's pretty smart," Dayo responded.

"That explains all the Apple cards I get for my birthday and Christmas," Leo remarked.

"Quit complaining! At least she gets you something!"

"But do we really have to go? I mean, how will it look to have an eighth grader go to a seventh grader's house?"

"There's gonna be a few eighth graders there," Dayo said. "Probably most of the soccer team." And then she gasped. "That means Joey Ramos and his friends will be there, too."

"I'm not going," Leo said flatly.

"Yes, you are," Harper responded. "And don't worry about Joey and his friends. I'll take care of them."

* * *

After school, while Harper was practicing with Leo and Dayo, Mrs. Devereux came to see them. As soon as she appeared, Leo fell backward and let out a scream.

"Calm down, young man, I'm not going to hurt you," Mrs. Devereux said.

"I . . . I . . . I'm . . . s-s-sorry," Leo stuttered.

Michael came running down from his room. "What happened to Leo?"

"Well, hello, little one." Mrs. Devereux smiled.

"Hi, Mrs. D! How are you?" Michael said with a big toothy grin. "Have you been with Grandma? How is she? I miss her."

"I know you do," Mrs. Devereux replied. "And she misses you so much. But she's doing well, and hopefully she'll be home in another month."

"That's good!" Michael sat on the armchair. "Whatcha doing?"

"Just talking," Harper said. "But don't you want to go watch your Adventure Buddies show? Isn't it on now?"

"Oh boy! I'm gonna go downstairs to watch it!"

Without a second glance, Michael ran to the basement, where their father had installed a big movie theater setup for their large screen television, right next to a playroom. It looked really nice now, but Harper could still never go down there. She really hated basements ever since the past summer, when she'd been trapped down there and had to relive her worst nightmare.

"Let's continue," Mrs. Devereux said. "The moon will reach peak fullness at eleven twenty-seven p.m. tomorrow night. That is when the witch will begin her transformation spell. We must start our plan five minutes before."

"Not any earlier?"

"No, we cannot risk warning the witch or the demon beforehand," Mrs. Devereux answered. "Before that time, the three of you will be positioned near the shop, ready for the binding ritual to capture the demon. The witch will be distracted preparing for her ritual and will expect the demon to keep watch. At exactly eleven twenty-two, Harper will enter the astral plane, distract the demon, and have him follow her. As soon as Harper is back in her body, Dayo and Leo will begin the binding. Once the demon is destroyed, you must quickly rush into the shop and find Kelly. Harper, it will be up to you to break the spell at the exact right moment. Does everyone understand what they are supposed to do?"

The three teens nodded grimly.

"Good, but we will still go over it a couple of more times."

After several more run-throughs, Mrs. Devereux told Leo and Dayo they were ready. Leo went downstairs to watch television with Michael, and Dayo went home.

Alone with Harper, she continued to push her, challenging her mental wall. She sent things flying at Harper randomly to test Harper's reflexes. Only when she was completely satisfied did she let Harper rest.

"Harper, none of us know what is going to happen tomorrow," Mrs. Devereux said. "It is up to you to be as prepared as possible for anything. Understand?"

"Yes, ma'am."

"Whatever happens, Harper, your grandmama and I are proud of you."

Harper was in the astral plane again. Her body was being pulled along quickly until she suddenly popped out into Jeune. It was empty. The shelves, usually stocked with makeup supplies and samples, were completely empty. Someone was humming in a low, throaty voice. She didn't recognize the melody, but it sounded old-timey. The sound called to her. She floated toward it despite a terror that crept up her throat. In the darkness of the store, she could make out a figure with dark hair moving small boxes filled with the youth beads.

There was something familiar about the form. Was it her sister? It didn't sound like her. Harper approached closer when, suddenly, the figure turned, and Harper reeled back in shock. In front of her stood someone who looked just like her, except with unnaturally green eyes.

"Hello, Harper," the other Harper said, facing her. And then she recognized the voice. It was that of Jenna.

Gasping for breath, Harper bolted awake. "It was just a dream! It was just a dream!"

She sat up and wrapped her arms around her legs, pulling herself into a tight ball. The sensation of being in the astral plane had felt very real, but she knew it was a dream because she was not pulled back into her body.

"But what does that mean?" she whispered. "How could it be me?"

Harper, your dreams are important. You have to listen to them.

She could hear her good friend Rose's voice in her head, and her heart tightened in pain. Rose, her oldest friend, who she'd lost to that horrible soul eater, the one who had eaten all the spirits at the cemetery of Our Lady of Mercy. Harper missed Rose so much.

Your dreams are trying to tell you something.

"What is it, Rose? What am I missing?"

You're in danger, Harper!

Harper jumped out of bed with both worry and excitement. She'd heard Rose's voice. Not just a memory, but Rose herself. But when she searched her room, she was all alone.

"Rose, are you sending me a message? I really wish you were still here. I don't understand." Harper crawled back into bed, pulled her comforter over her head, and tried to sort it all out.

Think, Harper, think. The dream was a warning. Rose was sending a warning. She says I'm in danger. Maybe this is all a trap. But why?

Harper remembered her dream and gasped. "She wants *me*!"

THE DEMON ANDRAS
Friday

"Harper, I'm not going to be able to see you before you go to your party," her mom said. "But Mrs. Kim will come over early to take care of Michael. I'm going to ask Mrs. Kim to order dinner so you and Leo can eat before you leave, all right?"

"Okay, thanks, Mom!"

"Make sure to text me the address so I can come pick you up when you are done," Yuna said.

Harper froze. She hadn't thought of how they would get home.

"But aren't you working overnight again?" she asked.

"I think it would be nice to take a break," Yuna

said. "I'd like to come and get you."

"But what if we want to go home early? Can we call a ride share to take us home?"

"I guess so," Yuna replied hesitantly. "But call me first. I'd rather pick you up if I can."

Agreeing, Harper realized she'd have to talk to Dayo about what they should do.

At lunch, it was Dayo who asked Devon if it was still okay for them to come to his house for his birthday get-together.

"Sure." He smiled. "That's cool!"

"See? No problem," Dayo whispered to Harper.

"I'm pretty sure he wasn't even listening 'cause he was too busy staring at Maya," Harper responded. They both giggled.

Harper quickly told Dayo about her mom insisting she'd pick them up.

"I think this all works out! Devon's house is in the neighborhood right behind the shopping mall. I looked at the map, and it is, like, a five- to ten-minute walk over to Jeune. My mom can give us a ride to Devon's, and when we're done at Jeune, we can walk back there and have your mom pick us up."

"Or she can pick us up with Kelly at Jeune," Harper said. "Kelly's going to need a ride home also."

"Either way, we'll be close enough that it won't be a problem."

"This is all working out," Harper said in relief. "I know we can do this. We will stop Jenna and save Kelly. We must."

Even though she believed what she said, Harper was still deeply afraid and worried.

It's okay, we can do this.

At eight o'clock, Mrs. Clayton drove with Dayo to pick up Harper and Leo.

"Have a great time, kids," Mrs. Clayton said after pulling in front of Devon's.

Devon's house was huge. Harper had heard that Devon's father was the CEO of some big company, and his mother was a reporter on the local news station. Walking into the house, Harper was surprised to see how many kids were there.

"I thought this was supposed to be a small get-together," Harper said.

Dayo shrugged. "I guess this is small to Devon."

They were greeted by Devon's parents, who were very nice and pointed them toward the refreshments before heading upstairs.

"You kids have a good time, don't do anything that'll make me mad, and remember we're upstairs if you need us," Devon's father boomed.

In the expansive living room, there had to be thirty or more kids hanging out. Devon, as usual, was hovering near Maya, who was sitting with Judy.

"Happy birthday, Devon," Dayo said as she handed him a birthday card. "This one's from Harper, Leo, and me."

"Cool. Thanks, guys," Devon said with a smile.

Dayo and Harper sat on the couch next to Maya and Judy, who were talking about something that happened earlier in the night.

"Hey, Harper, doesn't your sister work at that makeup place, Jeune?"

"Yeah, she does," Harper responded warily. "Why? What's up?"

"Judy and I went there to do some shopping, and the staff was all acting really weird," Maya replied. "They were emptying the shelves of all their products. And when we asked what we could buy, no one answered us. I mean, who does that during the holidays?"

"Yeah, I think something fishy is going on there," Judy said. "Maybe somebody complained about their products and that's why they're moving them all out."

"I don't even think the stuff is any good. I can't figure out why people like it so much," Maya said.

Harper agreed. "Me too."

Suddenly, Dayo nudged Harper in the side. "Harper, look, it's Joey and his thugs, and they're cornering Leo."

Harper got up and walked over to where Joey and his three friends were laughing at Leo.

"What are you doing here, new guy?" Joey was saying. "Who invited you?"

He pushed Leo hard against the wall, and Harper could see from Leo's expression that it hurt.

"He was invited with me," Harper said.

"Who the hell are you?" Joey asked, turning his attention to Harper.

"I'm his cousin."

Joey looked from Leo to Harper and laughed. "Cousins? How can this white boy be your cousin, China girl?"

"I'm not Chinese; I'm Korean. And I don't have to explain anything to you."

Joey sneered and was about to say something more when Harper lost her temper. With a wiggle of her finger, Joey's pants fell down, exposing his tighty-whities.

Everyone around them began to laugh, and some even took photos.

"What the . . . !" Joey grabbed at his pants, but

with another wiggle of her finger, Harper tripped Joey, and he fell down on his face. The laughter exploded, and even his friends couldn't help but laugh. Stumbling to his feet and finally pulling his pants back up, Joey ran out of the house without another word.

"Harper, that wasn't very nice," Leo said in a low voice. "But thank you."

Harper looked at him and took him by the arm. "Come meet my friends."

A few hours later, Harper was dying to leave. But she could see that both Dayo and Leo were having a good time. Leo had found a few eighth-grade friends and they were bonding over their love of comic books and anime. Harper wished she had a knack for making small talk with people, but it was something she had no interest in and wasn't really good at. After the first questions, Harper would just run out of things to say. It amazed her that Dayo and Leo were so good at it and could draw people out to talk for so long. It was definitely a talent. After checking her phone for the hundredth time, Harper saw it was time to leave.

"Guys, it's eleven. I think we should start walking over," Harper said.

They quickly said their good-byes and left the house. Out on the sidewalk, the streetlights were on, keeping the street well lit.

"Are you sure it's safe?" Leo asked nervously. "We've never been out this late alone."

"We're not alone. We have each other," Harper said sharply.

"You know what I mean," Leo responded. "No adults."

"I'm here," Mrs. Devereux said, suddenly appearing in front of them.

Leo gasped loudly. "I wish you would warn us before you do that!"

The spirit adviser smiled, as if she enjoyed scaring Leo just a little bit. Harper would have laughed if she wasn't so nervous.

"Stay close to me. I'm going to lead you to the back of the shop," Mrs. Devereux said. Tonight the spirit was wearing an emerald-green dress with white lace accents. Dayo sighed in admiration.

"If I ever go into fashion, I want to re-create these amazing old dresses," Dayo said. "They are so beautiful."

"Harper, I really like your friend," Mrs. Devereux responded over her shoulder. "She has excellent taste."

They followed the spirit to the corner and turned toward the bright lights of the major thoroughfare only a block away.

"Wow, Devon really does live close to the shopping mall," Harper remarked.

Instead of going down the street, Mrs. Devereux turned into a cobblestone alleyway that led them to the back of Jeune. Unlike the weird but imposing purple-and-black Victorian design of the front, the back of the house looked old and run-down. There was a high fenced backyard with a driveway and a large, very expensive black SUV parked in it. They unlatched the fence and entered a badly overgrown yard with a huge pile of boxes overflowing their large containers. The back of the house was completely dark, except for some dim lights from the main floor.

"Sit behind the vehicle and they won't be able to see you from the house," Mrs. Devereux said.

They sat in a circle on the grass. Harper checked the time. It was now 11:11. She quickly put out the bowls and holy water and placed the bells in front of Dayo and Leo.

"Salt!" Dayo said as she pulled out a container from her backpack and formed a thick circle of salt around them.

With the flick of her lighter, Harper started the purification procedure.

"Very good, as soon as Harper is in the astral plane, you must be ready for whatever happens,"

Mrs. Devereux said. "She will lead the demon back to this spot. As soon as that happens, you must begin the chant, first Leo and then Dayo, as quickly and quietly as possible."

The three friends grabbed each other's hands and squeezed them for comfort.

"Good luck, Harper," Dayo whispered.

"You can do this," Leo said.

Taking a deep breath, Harper closed her eyes and entered the astral plane.

The dim emptiness was now eerily familiar to Harper. As she slowly spun in a circle, she became aware of the dread that surrounded her as she sensed the demon's evil presence. The demon was very near, but it had not yet seen her. She needed to catch its attention quickly.

Your aura, Harper.

Harper could hear Rose's voice again. *It's like a magnetic call to any spiritual being in your immediate area. It's intensely bright and brilliant silvery-white.*

Yes, Mrs. Devereux had been teaching her to dim her aura, to control it at the right times. But here, in this vast darkness, her aura would be a clarion call to the demon. To do this, she would have to lower the walls in her mind and leave herself vulnerable. It was a terrible risk, but she had no choice.

"I can do this," Harper said out loud. "I am strong. I am powerful."

She lowered her shield, and the impact in the astral plane was immediate. She began to glow with a bright silvery light, illuminating the area.

"So this is how ghosts see me," Harper marveled, before sensing an evil presence.

"Do my eyes deceive me? Has a feast appeared before me like a gift?"

The red glowing eyes drew near. But now with Harper's aura glowing so bright, she could finally see the rest of its demonic figure. He had the form of a man, even wearing what looked like a designer suit, but his face was anything but human. He reminded her of a Japanese oni mask she'd once seen in a museum. Onis were Japanese demon monsters with red faces and horns growing out of their forehead. This was exactly what the demon looked like.

Deliberately turning her back on the demon, Harper began floating away.

"Oh, no, not this time, little girl," the demon growled. "I have need of you tonight."

Looking over her shoulder, Harper saw the demon charging at her full speed. She turned around, and just as he grabbed for her, she forced herself into her body.

Opening her eyes, she saw the demon form floating right above their circle, looking surprised. Dayo and Leo had already started chanting and ringing the bells, and the demon began to curse.

"Release me or you will all die hideous deaths," he seethed as he strained against the binding spell.

Harper chanted loudly with the others. "Through the power of the Ancient One, I bind you. You will do no harm. Through the power of the Worthy One, I bind you. You will do no harm."

With each toll of the bell, Harper clapped her hands, and the sound rang out, causing the demon to stiffen in pain.

"Please release me, I'll grant you any wish. I'll make all your dreams come true. Whatever you want," the demon pleaded as his skin began to sear and crackle.

"Do not listen to his lies, children," Mrs. Devereux commanded.

The demon suddenly changed forms and turned into Kelly. "Harper! Stop it! You're hurting me! Why are you doing this? I'm your sister!"

Leo gasped and stopped chanting.

"No, Leo! That's not Kelly!"

But the demon immediately sensed Leo's weakness.

"Leo, honey, what are you doing?" The demon had changed form again, this time into Leo's mother. "Why do you keep causing problems? If it weren't for you, your father and I wouldn't be getting a divorce!"

"No, Leo! That's not your mom!" Harper shouted. The devastation on her cousin's face was painful to see.

"Leo, close your eyes and don't listen!" Dayo yelled; her own eyes were shut tight.

It was too late. Harper could see Leo's hand stop ringing the bell as if it were in slow motion. She lunged for the bell, but the demon was faster. Leo's tragic expression changed to one of pure evil as the demon took possession.

"I like this body!" the demon crowed. "Now let's see what it can do."

Rising to his feet, he threw Wisdom over the backyard fence and kicked Truth out of Dayo's hands. Dayo fell backward in horror as Leo towered over her.

"Don't you dare touch her!" Harper used her powers to shove Leo out of the circle. Without hesitation, Dayo quickly poured salt around the broken borders.

The demon in Leo's body paced outside of their circle.

"Delightful, truly delightful, the mistress will be so ecstatic to see what I've ght for her!"

A sudden flash of light disoriented them as Mrs. Devereux made her presence known in a brilliant display of colors.

"I think you've got that a little backward," she drawled, her form glowing with a bright red aura. "Harper, the bells!"

Harper raised her arms and shouted, "Wisdom! Truth!"

The bells flew into her hands. She handed Truth to Dayo, and they immediately began chanting again.

"Oh, no, you don't!" The demon surged toward them, but without stopping her chant, Dayo sprayed Leo with holy water.

The demon shrieked and surged out of Leo's body. Harper used her powers to quickly lift her cousin's swaying form over the salt border and drop him in their circle.

Suspended high above them was the demon Andras once again in his true form.

"I'm me now, Harper," Leo said as he took back the Wisdom bell. "I can do it."

"Keep your eyes closed, guys. Don't look at him and don't listen," Harper said firmly.

Dayo and Leo closed their eyes and continued to chant and ring their bells. Harper kept her eyes open, took in a deep breath, and spread her arms wide, absorbing the energy around her. Forcefully exhaling, Harper clapped her hands together, releasing a powerful blast of energy on the demon. Andras screamed in anguish as his skin ripped open in gaping cracks, looking as if molten lava was trying to escape from within.

"Please spare me! I'll do anything you want!"

Ignoring his pleas, Harper blasted him one more time and watched as he imploded into nothingness. The bowls before them filled with black goo. Harper poured holy water and salt on the goo and watched it sizzle and evaporate.

"Well done," Mrs. Devereux remarked. "How did you figure that out?"

"It was Dayo's idea," Harper explained. "Instead of having to haul all the demon's remnants to running water or a cemetery, she figured out that these two pure things, holy water and salt, should cancel out the evil. And it worked."

"Excellent work, children," Mrs. Devereux said. "But the hardest part is next. Stay focused and be smart."

SAVING KELLY

They hurriedly packed up their things and followed Mrs. Devereux to the back door of the shop. The door was surprisingly unlocked. Entering through the back took them through the employee locker room and out into the store area. The store floor was completely dark. Even the pink neon lights that usually lit up the windows were all off.

"This place is so creepy," Leo whispered. "It's like a haunted house."

The main store area was empty. But Harper knew that Kelly and Jenna had to be in the house somewhere. She could sense the witch's presence. It was the heaviness of the energy around her that spoke of an evil waiting to pounce on her.

"Where are you?" Harper whispered.

A laugh echoed in the air. Dayo and Leo gripped Harper's arms tightly.

"Ow," Harper whispered.

Harper followed the sound to the same curtained doorway she'd been through previously. They entered the crowded storage room, which was filled with boxes of Jeune products, and exited through a side door that led to the small landing of a staircase. The laugh emanated from downstairs.

"The basement," Harper sighed. "Why does it always have to be the basement?"

Mrs. Devereux was visibly uneasy. The edges of her outline were flickering slightly, as if she were too distracted to hold her shape.

"There is something that is bothering me, Harper," she said. "It shouldn't be this easy to have gotten this far. Be extra cautious. It may be a trap."

Dayo squeezed Harper's arm tighter, and Leo's Adam's apple bobbed up and down in nervousness. Harper reached over and patted them both. "You're doing great, guys. Let's finish this."

The eerie laugh sounded again, as if it was mocking them. Harper took the lead as she walked cautiously down the stairs that creaked softly with each step. The stairwell opened directly into a poorly lit basement, with large mirrors lining two of its walls and shelves filled with boxes and supplies all along the far end of the room. The only bright light came from the large glass container Harper had seen in her vision. Small lights in the top box would zap into the lower box and then coalesce into a large colorful bead that dropped to the bottom chamber.

It was near the glass container that she spotted Kelly and Jenna staring at each other.

"What are they doing?" Dayo asked.

"Can they not hear us?" Leo asked.

"She's already cast her spell. Dayo, Leo, make a large circle of salt, quickly!" Mrs. Devereux commanded. "Stay within the circle, and ready your bells."

Dayo laid down a thick white circle of salt as Leo hurriedly pulled out the bowls and bells. Harper rushed forward to gaze at Jenna's eyes, but they remained the eerie bright green they always were.

"It's not time yet," Harper said.

Suddenly, Kelly started to choke. Her face turned bright red, and her hands were clawing at her neck, trying to pull off the cameo.

"Kelly!"

Leo and Dayo tried to move, but Mrs. Devereux

yelled at them to stay in the circle.

"Harper, pull her into the circle!"

She dragged her sister to Dayo and Leo.

"Close the circle, quickly!"

Dayo resalted the area where Kelly's feet broke the circle, while Leo tried to pull the cameo off.

"Ow! It's burning hot!" Leo snatched his hand back in pain.

Harper could see heat rising from where the cameo was searing into Kelly's neck.

"Dayo and Leo, use the bells!" Mrs. Devereux shouted. Suddenly, she screamed, "Harper watch ou—" Her voice cut out completely.

Harper looked up in horror to see Jenna capturing the spirit adviser in a glass ball.

"Well, well, well, look at this witch ghost I've caught." Jenna smirked.

"Harper, what do we do?" Dayo wailed.

"Start the chant," she said. Concentrating on the glass ball, Harper yanked it out of Jenna's hand and caught it in her own. Harper immediately put it in her coat pocket and zipped it closed. She'd worry about Mrs. Devereux later.

"Bravo, Harper!" Jenna smiled. "I've been waiting for you. I'm so excited to see what else you can do, little witch."

"I'm not a witch. I'm a spirit hunter," Harper growled.

"What you will be is the greatest witch in the world," Jenna corrected. She crooked her finger and Harper came flying across the room, until she stopped right in front of the witch. Harper tried to move to fight her, but Jenna whispered some words that froze her in place.

Behind them, Harper could hear Dayo and Leo begin to ring the bells and chant again.

Jenna turned her head to look at them and laughed. "Oh, your friends are adorable! Little wannabe shamans. I'm not sure what the bells do, but I doubt they can save your sister." She gave a fake frown. "Poor Kelly. I really liked her."

"Let my sister go." Harper managed to spit the words out through her clenched teeth.

"I'm afraid I can't do that. Your friends have surrounded themselves with salt, and my magic is powerless to cross it. But if you tell them to step out of the circle, I'm sure I can help them."

Dayo and Leo had stopped chanting in confusion. Immediately, Kelly began choking hard again.

"Don't listen to her!" Harper yelled.

The bells and chanting continued again, and Kelly

wheezed, as if the pressure was easing on her throat.

"How long do you think your friends can keep it up? They're going to get tired eventually." Jenna smirked.

"What do you want, witch?" Harper asked.

The witch's green eyes glowed feverishly. "I think you know."

"What do you want with me?" Harper was desperate to stall.

"When Andras first told me about you, I thought he was lying, which, let's face it, demons do all the time," Jenna said. "A powerful child who could break the cycle of my curse and allow me to retain one form for eternity? How can there be such a creature? But then I saw you with my own eyes twice, first on the day of the makeovers, and then the day I gave your sister the cameo. I could see your aura glowing in that dark room. So beautiful. Your energy force is incredibly strong. When Andras said he saw you in the astral plane, I could not believe it. A miracle that I had been searching for, for years!"

Her green eyes widened as she stared at Harper with greedy desire. "You are perfect. A vessel of pure energy, powerful enough to move through the astral and physical planes." Jenna turned Harper's face from side to side as Harper watched helplessly. "Not bad-looking, either, with lots of potential. The answer to all my problems."

Harper's dream had been right. It had never been Kelly who was the witch's target. It had been Harper she'd been after all along. She'd given the cameo to Kelly only after she'd seen Harper at the makeover event. After the demon had told her about Harper's abilities. This had all been a trap, and Kelly was the bait. Sheer rage flooded through Harper, blotting out the fear that had been rising within.

"Don't you need the cameo?" Harper asked.

"Why, yes, I do," Jenna said in surprise. "Andras, get me my cameo."

When there was no response, Jenna frowned in earnest.

"Andras? The cameo, now."

It was Harper's turn to smile. "Andras is not here anymore. We made sure of that."

A flicker of annoyance crossed Jenna's flawless complexion. She left Harper hanging in the air and strode purposefully over to where the others were protecting Kelly.

"Stop this incessant noise immediately!" Jenna shouted.

"Ring the bells harder!" Harper screamed.

A cacophony of ringing made Jenna shriek and cover her ears. In sheer rage, Jenna sent a heavy cabinet flying toward them.

"No!" Harper focused her power on harnessing all the energy in the room and caught the cabinet, sending it crashing into the wall instead. But the damage was done, the circle of salt was broken, and Jenna leaned over and snatched the cameo off Kelly's neck.

As soon as the cameo was off, Kelly woke up crying in pain. "What's happening?"

"Let them go, and I'll do what you want," Harper said. "But if you hurt them, I'll make it as difficult as possible, and it might take all night."

Jenna's green eyes assessed Harper's expression. They flickered down to see Dayo and Leo hovering protectively over a shocked Kelly.

"Very well. They may go."

"No, Harper! We can't leave you!" Dayo said.

"Take Kelly and go," Harper responded.

"Go now, children, before I change my mind," Jenna said in a pleasant voice, tinged with malevolence.

With agonized looks, Dayo and Leo helped Kelly to her feet and dragged her to the stairs.

"Why are we leaving Harper? We can't leave her!" Kelly protested, but she was too weak to fight them.

Jenna and Harper remained absolutely still, until they heard the slam of the back door. Only then did Jenna approach Harper and put the cameo necklace around her neck.

"Your friends are loyal and brave," she said. "Too bad I'll have to take care of them when this is all over."

The rage inside of Harper surged. "I warned you not to hurt my friends."

"You shouldn't have brought them into this. Then it would have only been your family I'd have to kill off," Jenna drawled. "After all, a poor orphan girl who is adopted into my estate makes far more sense than one with an inconvenient family."

At that moment, the rage that was building inside of her exploded in a fury, and Harper let it loose in a howl so loud it shook the house. Instantly, she was freed as the blast sent Jenna hurling to the other side of the room and shattered the glass containers filled with the youth beads.

"Nooo! My precious beads! You'll pay for this, girl!"

But this time Harper was ready for her, hurling boxes and bottles and vases at the witch. Jenna knocked most out of the air with just a wave of her hands, but Harper was bombarding her with everything in the room that wasn't nailed down. Every time Jenna tried to chant a spell, Harper sent something flying at her face.

Jenna screamed in frustration and blasted at Harper with electric bolts that shot out of her hands. Instinctively, Harper pulled two large mirrors off the walls and used them as shields to deflect the electricity, sending them sparking every which way. Holding the mirrors like cymbals, Harper smashed them into the witch, but when the mirrors shattered, Jenna was gone.

At full alert, Harper searched the basement. Small fires had broken out in several parts of the basement where Jenna's electricity had hit. Broken glass and boxes littered the floor. But still no Jenna.

Harper could feel her in the room, the malevolent presence that seemed to suck up all the air. Channeling all her senses, Harper listened and felt the air change just as Jenna charged at her. Whirling out of the way, Harper used the air to blast Jenna away from her, sending her soaring into a cabinet. A large glass jar was knocked off the top and smashed into Jenna's head. She collapsed to the ground.

The downed body broke through Harper's anger, and she dropped all that she'd been about to throw. Jenna was motionless, blood pouring from her head.

Is she dead? No, that wasn't enough to kill her, Harper thought.

Approaching Jenna cautiously, Harper leaned down to see if she was still breathing. A clawlike hand gouged at Harper's neck, threatening to cut off her breathing. Jenna stood up, lifting Harper off her feet with inhuman strength. Her face was covered in blood, and her eyes were maniacal.

"I will have your body," she sneered.

The cameo around Harper's neck grew red hot and burned her skin as if it were molten lava. Harper clawed at it, desperate to get it off and stop the pain.

Whatever you do, don't open your mouth!

Harper heard Mrs. Devereux's voice in her head. She squeezed her eyes tight as she pulled at the cameo. The jewelry felt like it had melted into her skin.

"Look at me, Harper!"

The pain was excruciating, and Harper couldn't hold back the screams that ripped from her throat.

You have to break free of her hold! Use your powers!

"I can't, I can't," Harper sobbed. The pain was too much for her. She could feel herself blacking out, her soul beginning to separate from her body. "I'm sorry!"

"Leave my daughter alone, you monster!"

Harper was stunned to hear her mother's voice. Opening her eyes, she saw Yuna slam a step stool into the back of Jenna's head. The claw around Harper's neck loosened, and she fell to the ground. Harper could see that Jenna's eyes had turned completely black. Without a moment to lose, Harper jumped to her feet and forced a hand mirror to come flying into her hand. As she quickly held it up to Jenna's face, she watched as the black eyes in the mirror slowly turned a glassy green.

"No, what have you done?!" Jenna gasped. She tried to cover her mouth with her hands, but black vapor poured out of her mouth and was absorbed into the mirror.

"Mom! Stay away!" Harper shouted. She saw Yuna step back into the relative safety of the staircase, the step stool still gripped tightly in her hands.

Harper raced over to where Dayo and Leo had left her bells, clearing the space of all the items that had fallen over them. Placing the mirror on the ground, she began to chant and ring her bells. As the witch's body lurched toward Harper, her outstretched hands began turning into skeletal claws.

"Through the power of the Ancient One, I bind you. You will do no harm. Through the power of the Worthy One, I bind you. You will do no harm," Harper chanted with every ring of Wisdom and Truth.

The witch's body began to disintegrate. Skin

melted away to bloody flesh until it, too, decayed to nothing but bones. Her face melted into a dull white skull. The form finally collapsed to the ground and then turned into a large mound of dust. As Harper stared in shock at the dust on the ground, the burning around her neck began to dissipate. Then she put a hand to her neck and realized the cameo was gone.

Harper looked down at the mirror, and on top of it there was nothing but a dark, tar-like residue that bubbled. She reached into her bag and pulled out a bottle of holy water, which she poured over the residue. It made a loud crackling, sizzling sound and dissipated. Only then did Harper sag in relief.

"Harper, are you okay?"

Her mother pulled Harper away from the nightmarish scene and hugged her tight.

"Come on, we have to get out of here! It's dangerous."

Before they could leave, Harper stopped. "Wait, Mom, I need my bells."

Yuna hurriedly gathered the bowls and bells, threw them in the bag, and rushed to take Harper upstairs and out of the house, just as the basement erupted into fire. They headed to the back door and found Dayo, Leo, and Kelly in the backyard. As soon as they saw Harper, they all cried out in relief. But

Yuna urged them out into the alleyway, where she'd left her car. After calling the fire department, Yuna started the engine and began driving immediately.

"Mom, how did you know to come?" Harper asked once they were safely away.

"Michael called me. He said he had a dream and told me to go to Jeune through the back entrance and down to the basement. He said you were in trouble."

"Michael?" Harper was shocked.

Yuna nodded. "And then, on my way here, your grandmother called me frantic with worry and said the exact same thing."

Harper could see that her mother's hands were gripping the steering wheel so tightly that her knuckles shone white in the reflection of the streetlights.

"Thanks, Mom. You saved me."

Yuna swallowed several times before replying. "If everyone is all right, let's talk about it when we get home."

Dayo reached over from behind to hug Harper tight.

SAFE AT HOME

Back at Harper's house, Yuna paid the babysitter and walked her out. Kelly was so tired that she went straight to bed, but Harper, Dayo, and Leo sat at the kitchen table, waiting for Yuna to return.

"What happened, Harper?" Leo asked. "How'd you escape?"

"Mom came in and hit Jenna on the head with a step stool," Harper relayed. "She'd been trying to switch bodies with me, and I saw that her eyes were black, so I used the mirror and . . ." Harper shuddered.

Yuna came in and collapsed onto a chair. She ran a shaky hand through her hair.

"Well, I need to catch my breath! Is everyone okay? Who wants some hot chocolate?" Yuna asked.

"Yes, please!" Dayo said.

Leo and Harper nodded.

The act of warming up milk and getting snacks seemed to calm Yuna. She placed three mugs of hot cocoa with marshmallows and a plate of cookies in front of them. Then she sat down next to Harper, grabbed her hand, and said, "Please. Start from the beginning."

It took a good hour to tell Harper's mother everything that happened, and they had to call Grandma Lee to explain, too. At the end, Harper pulled out the glass ball with Mrs. Devereux captured within it.

"Grandma, how do I free her?" Harper asked.

"All you have to do is think her free," she answered simply.

Think her free? Harper closed her eyes and imagined the crystal ball. *Mrs. Devereux, I release you.*

"Well, that's a relief! Thank you, Harper," Mrs. Devereux said.

At her appearance, Leo startled again, but Dayo and Harper were relieved to see her.

"Are you all right, Mrs. Devereux?" Harper asked.

"Yes, I am fine, and I am so proud of you all. And so surprised at your mother, Harper," Mrs. Devereux responded. "She was a force to reckon with."

"She saved me," Harper said simply.

"Yes, she surely did."

Yuna looked puzzled. "Who are you talking to?"

Harper reached over to hold her mother's hand. Yuna's eyes grew wide and her mouth fell open in shock as Mrs. Devereux appeared before her.

"Mom, this is Mrs. Devereux, Grandma's adviser and a very powerful spirit," Harper said.

Yuna's grip tightened painfully on Harper's hand. "How is this happening?"

"It is because your daughter is a powerful shaman," Mrs. Devereux explained. "Probably the strongest I've ever seen."

Harper could sense her mother's fear. "Mrs. Devereux is the reason we were able to save Kelly."

Immediately, Yuna stood up, still holding Harper's hand, and bowed deeply. "Thank you so much for saving my children."

"Your mother is one of the few humans who I care for in the world and count on as my dear friend. And I have come to care for her offspring just as much," Mrs. Devereux replied. "It is my pleasure and my honor to help them."

The spirit turned to Harper. "I must go now. I

know your grandmama is very anxious, and I should go to her."

After the ghost left, they said good night to Grandma Lee on the phone and got ready to go to bed. Yuna hugged each of them tightly. When it came to Harper, Yuna started tearing up.

"Harper, I wish you had told me earlier what was happening," she whispered. "This was too huge a responsibility to put on your shoulders alone. I don't know what your grandmother was thinking."

"Grandma was thinking that I'm a lot stronger than you think," Harper replied. "And when I needed help, she sent you."

"Michael sent me," Yuna replied in wonderment. "How did he know?"

"Michael is strong also," Harper said. "It runs in the family."

"This power that you have," Yuna said hesitantly. "How will it affect you? Can you still be a normal girl and enjoy life? Must you always be in danger?"

"Mom, let's not worry about that now," Harper replied.

As they were heading up to bed, Harper's dad came home, completely oblivious to the mood of the room.

"Good night, kids! Don't forget, brunch at ten!"

Yuna burst into tears and embraced her husband.

"What did I say?" he asked in bewilderment.

In Harper's room, Dayo and Harper prepared for bed. They got into their sleeping bags next to each other and turned off the lights.

"I'm so tired, I don't know if I can get up at ten."

"We have to," Harper replied. "Otherwise he's going to sulk all day and complain about how we ruined his brunch."

Dayo groaned. "He just got home. Won't he be too tired?"

Harper giggled. "Nope."

They faced each other, and Harper reached over to hold Dayo's hand.

"Thank you for being there with me," she said. "I'm so grateful you are my friend."

"Me too," Dayo replied.

"Good night, best friend."

"Sleep tight, best friend."

KELLY BACK TO NORMAL

At eight a.m., Michael came storming into Harper's room and jumped between them.

"Wake up, wake up! I had a dream last night and I told Mommy and she saved you, right?"

Harper woke up to Michael's bouncing and immediately hugged him.

"Yes, you saved me! How did you know?"

"In my dream, I saw Grandma, but she couldn't see me. She was so worried about you, and she was crying. She said you were in terrible trouble and that Mommy had to go to Kelly's work right away, before it was too late. She said to go to the back entrance and down to the basement. So I got up and asked Mrs. Kim to call Mommy for me. I did good, right?"

"You did great, Michael!"

"Don't forget, you said you would do anything I want this weekend!"

"I remember. What did you want to do?"

"You have to play with me all day long!"

"Deal!"

"Yippee!"

A loud groan came from Dayo, who had zipped herself completely into her sleeping bag.

"Michael, can you let me sleep some more?" Dayo asked in a muffled voice.

Giggling, Michael and Harper put their fingers to their lips and shushed each other.

"Let's go check on Kelly," Harper whispered.

The two walked over to Kelly's room and slid open the door. They were both surprised to see Kelly sitting up in bed, crying.

"Kelly, what's the matter?" Michael asked. He ran right over to her bed and climbed in to give her a hug.

Kelly put out her other arm and gestured for Harper to come join them.

"I'm so sorry, guys," she said as she hugged them

tight. "I woke up early and talked with Mom and Grandma. It's really hard to believe I was under a spell, but it explains everything I was going through. I was such a jerk."

"You were very mean to Mommy and Daddy," Michael chided.

"Yeah, I know. I was a terror."

"It's okay, Kelly," Harper said. "You weren't yourself."

"I just can't believe Jenna was a witch and trying to steal my body."

Harper just nodded. No need to tell her that she wasn't the real target. No need for her to feel more guilty than she already did.

"Thank you for saving me, Harper."

"It wasn't just me," Harper replied. "Dayo, Leo, Grandma, and Mom all helped. We all did it together."

"Me too, me too! I helped!" Michael piped up.

"And Michael." Harper smiled. "He called Mom and got her to us just in the nick of time."

"I'm going downstairs to watch my shows. Don't disturb me," Michael announced.

The girls laughed. He sounded just like their grandma when she wanted to watch her K-dramas.

After he left, Kelly asked Harper for more details on everything that had happened. When she was done, Kelly was quiet and pale.

"What an evil woman," she said.

"Technically an evil witch," Harper countered.

"What happened to her? Mom didn't really know."

"Once her soul was captured in the mirror and destroyed, the body began to age rapidly. I didn't quite understand, but Grandma said that although the Jenna body was only forty years old, it had housed a spirit that was over four hundred years old. So when it was emptied, it disintegrated into dust."

"So she's definitely gone?"

"Definitely!"

"That's a relief. What happened to the cameo?"

"I think when the witch disappeared, so did the cameo, because it was a cursed object."

Kelly shuddered. Climbing out of bed, she walked over to her vanity. She took all her Jeune products and dumped them into her garbage bin.

"That makes me feel much better," she said. "But now I'm going to have to buy more makeup. Do you want to go to the mall with me?"

Harper jumped to her feet, shaking her head. "Uh-uh, no way. I hate shopping!"

Kelly laughed and rushed over to give Harper a big hug.

"I love you, little sis!"

"Little? I'm a head taller than you!"

"You can be six feet tall and you're still going to be my little sister!"

EPILOGUE
Saturday afternoon, a week later

Harper's parents had taken Michael to a tae kwon do exhibition at his school. Leo was ensconced in Peter's armchair reading comic books, and Harper was raiding the pantry for snacks when Dayo came over.

"Hey, Dayo! What's up?" Leo said as he opened the door.

"Where's Harper?"

"I'm in the kitchen," Harper called out.

Dayo came running in, dragging Leo behind her. "Have you guys been following the news?" she asked.

"Uh-uh. What happened?" Leo asked.

"Okay, first of all, the fire chief is saying that the

suspicious fire that burned down the shop was most likely deliberately set," Dayo said.

"Well, they got that one wrong," Harper replied. "Jenna was shooting electric bolts around, and it was sparking everywhere. Nothing deliberate about it."

"I think they mean that it wasn't an accident," Leo clarified.

"Okay, well, that's sort of true, although I don't think Jenna meant to burn the shop down."

Dayo waved her hands in the air to get their attention again.

"But that's not all! The FDA found that Jeune's entire new beauty line is full of cancer-causing toxins, and they want them all recalled."

"Great news!" Harper crowed. "I'm so glad those products will be off the market! Although I'm pretty sure they can't steal youth anymore, since the witch is dead. Also, while all the products in the shop were destroyed, there was still that factory in Baltimore, right? So does that mean the FDA will confiscate it?"

"I don't know! But there's even more!" Dayo sputtered. "The police are searching for the owner, Jenna Graham, who is wanted in connection with an investigation of the twenty-year-old murder of the previous owner, Martha Greenstein. Graham was a young assistant of Greenstein's who went on to become the head of a huge corporation, with no experience. They said that they recently discovered papers that show there might be truth in the rumor that Graham killed Greenstein for ownership of C. Wentworth, Inc. Greenstein, who was the sole shareholder of C. Wentworth, signed over all her ownership interest to Jenna Graham, on the same day of Greenstein's mysterious death."

"Well, we know that's all true, except not the way they think it went down."

"They said they've been looking for Graham, but no one has seen her since Friday night," Dayo continued. She paused and looked at Harper. "Wouldn't they have found traces of her in the fire?"

"The thing is, she turned to absolute dust. I can't remember what happened to her clothing, but I'm pretty sure it would have all burned up," Harper replied. "There would be nothing left to find."

"So, this will all turn into a great mystery only we will know the truth about," Dayo said. "That's pretty cool."

"Even if we told the truth, no one would ever believe us," Leo responded. He paused. "Seriously, who would believe us?"

"Guys, sometimes *I* can't believe everything that's

happened!" Dayo laughed. "And, Harper, you're like a superhero!"

"Ew, no, don't say that! My mom and dad had to give me a whole lecture about how I must only use my powers for good and never use them except in an emergency. It was pretty awkward, superhero-origin-story stuff and all. I wanted to disappear."

Her parents had had a long talk with her about the dangers of having such extraordinary powers and how it was important for her to hide them from people in order to live as ordinary a life as possible.

"Besides, I have no interest in being some kind of crime-fighting superhero," Harper said. "What I am is a spirit hunter. We all are! We fight the evil others can't see!"

She smiled at her friends. "Hey, that was pretty catchy! Maybe it should be our team slogan."

Dayo laughed while Leo groaned.

At that moment, Harper's phone buzzed.

"Hey, I got a text from Olivia!"

Olivia Bennington was the daughter of the Bennington hotel chain's owner. They'd all become friends when they were vacationing at Razu Island and saved Olivia from the monsters there.

"What did she say?" Dayo asked.

"'Hi, Harper, can you and Dayo come visit me in NYC over Christmas break? There are ghosts in my building. Need your help.'"

"Oh, New York City! I've always wanted to go!" Dayo said.

"Hey, she doesn't mention me!" said Leo, visibly peeved.

Harper tapped her lip. "My parents were going to take all of us to my aunt's house to visit Grandma and the new baby for Christmas anyway. Maybe your parents will let you come with us, Dayo?"

Dayo clapped her hands in excitement. "NYC ghosts! How scary do you think they'll be?"

"Oh, I bet they're really bad, but I know we can take 'em."

"I'm pretty sure you'll be the scariest thing they've ever seen, Harper," Leo said with a grin.

"Then let's go kick some NYC ghost butts!"

ACKNOWLEDGMENTS

Spirit Hunters 3:
Something Wicked
Presented by HarperCollins Children's Books

Written by Ellen TheOdious Oh

Brilliant Editor Extraordinaire—Alyson Day
Best Amazing Agent—Marietta Zacker
Fantastic Assistant Editor—Eva Lynch-Comer
Marvelous Copy Editors—Jacqueline Hornberger,
Kathryn Silsand, Chelsea Cohen, and Susan
Bishansky

Greatest Art Director—Joel Tippie
Phenomenal Cover Artist—Matt Rockefeller

Fabulous Harper Team—Delaney Heisterkamp and
Jacqueline Burke
The Big Genius Boss Lady—Suzanne Murphy

Special Thanks to These Awesome People:
Olugbemisola "Gbemi Rocks!" Rhuday-Perkovich

Dhonielle "Badass" Clayton
Caroline "My Savior" Richmond
Breanna "Bubbly Bre" McDaniel
Hena "Eating Buddy" Khan

Dream Team Oh:
Summer "I Object" Oh
Skye "Ogres Are Like Onions" Oh
Graysin Sun "Ate Bees" Oh
Be Careful He Bites Tokki
Loves Everyone Kiko
Husband and Best Friend Sonny "Meow Meow" Oh

Thank you to all my dear readers everywhere!